FICTION

INQUIRIES & ADVERTISING

Address: Suite 22, 509 Commissioners Road West, London, Ontario, N6J 1Y5
Advertising: Email info@mysterymagazine.ca
Editor: Kerry Carter **Publisher:** Chuck Carter **Cover Artist:** Robin Grenville Evans
Submissions: https://mysterymagazine.ca/submit.asp
Mystery Magazine is published monthly by AM Marketing Strategies. The stories in this magazine are all fictitious, and any resemblance between the characters in them and actual persons is completely coincidental. Reproduction or use, in any manner of editorial or pictorial content without express written permission is prohibited. Copyright on stories remain with the artist or author. No portion of this magazine or its cover may be reproduced without the artist's or author's permission.

GOLDEN GRIFFINS

Jenny Blackford

Mother and I had strolled almost the whole way from our farmhouse down to the agora near the harbor, when everything started to go wrong.

It was always a relief to get out of the house, and away from our endless women's work of spinning and weaving—even if Mother walked so maddeningly slowly, while I tried to hurry us along. Our small expedition was officially to buy fresh tuna and asparagus for the family's dinner, some dates and almonds for later, and maybe some honey cakes for a snack. But I had an ulterior motive for asking to go shopping with my mother that day: the golden griffin earrings that I'd seen the day before at the jeweler's stall. They were little half-arches of silver, with tiny flying griffins in shining gold dangling from each of them. There was only one pair, and my life would never be the same if I missed out on them.

Could I *really* have met griffins near our farm when I was younger, or was that just my over-active imagination? The famous historian Herodotus wrote that griffins guarded their gold from the one-eyed Arimaspians far away in the north-west of Scythia—not here in Athens. What would a golden-winged griffin have been doing near our farmhouse? But the griffin earrings were the most beautiful things that I'd ever seen, except for the griffins—if they were real, not just my imagination.

Then Mother said, "I've been thinking, Apollonia. It's only two or three streets out of our way to call in at Philoumene's house for a few minutes."

The extra distance out of our way was more like thirteen streets than three, of course. And it was already close to midday. In that few minutes, someone else would probably buy the earrings that I yearned for. Our local agora here near the sea-port was tiny compared with the big one near the Acropolis in the city, but it was always busy. I couldn't help groaning, but I tried not to let Mother see or hear. Philoumene had been her best friend since they were both toddlers. They always acted as if they had years of conversation to catch up on, not days, or sometimes only hours. But what if Philoumene's appalling mother-in-law was still visiting?

As we stood at the front door, Mother whispered, "Remember not to mention the slave boy who died. It's a bit of a sore point with Philoumene."

"What? Pistos? But he was perfectly healthy." And I'd liked him. He and his father were captured by pirates while they were sailing from Corinth to one of the towns in Sicily on business. The pirates stole all their property and sold them as slaves.

"Weren't you listening the other day? Pistos stole a cloak, so Philoumene's husband beat him, and he died. Philoumene wasn't happy."

"Oh … But why would he steal a cloak? Where could he possibly hide it?"

The heavy door that led to the courtyard opened, and the young red-haired slave girl Eirene let us through. Philoumene rushed down the wooden stairs from her room up in the women's quarters, squealing with delight. "Oh, Demetria, and little Apollonia, how lovely to see you!"

I bristled inside. At sixteen, I was hardly "little"—even if my father hadn't yet married me off to someone twice my age. All the girls I knew were already married to old men their fathers ate and drank with. Some of them had popped out babies or were well on the way towards it, providing heirs for the families they'd married into. Maybe none of my father's friends were interested in me. Maybe I wasn't pretty enough for him to marry off easily, even with the dowry that would go with me. But even if I had any say in the matter—which I didn't—I was in no hurry for marriage and baby-making. There were so many interesting things in the world. Griffins, for a start.

Of course, Philoumene meant no harm. She never meant any harm. She just opened her mouth and words came out, with no actual thought process in between.

She wasn't ready for visitors—her hair was elaborately done, but she wasn't made up. There were no nets or circlets on her head to hold her hair in place, and no bracelets jangling on her arms, though rings shone on her plump fingers. Her old slave Geta ran down the stairs behind her, with Philoumene's baby boy on her hip. Geta looked exhausted, and the circles under her eyes were worse than I'd ever seen them. Perhaps the baby was teething again.

My mother and Philoumene chattered interminably on the other side of the courtyard while I wriggled with impatience. Even apart from the urgent business of the griffin earrings, I was starving! The sticky, crunchy coriander-seed-scented sesame cakes from the baker in the agora were starting to sound really good.

Instead, I was sitting in Philoumene's paved courtyard with nothing to do but watch the early spring sun climb higher and higher in the cloudless sky, while Mother and her friend talked and talked and talked. Old Geta rocked the precious boy baby to sleep in his wooden cradle, singing a lullaby in her own language from north of Macedon. Young red-headed Eirene sat quietly spinning handful after handful of combed fleece into thread far more efficiently than I would ever manage. The wool was dyed the most delicious-looking eggy yellow. It made me even hungrier.

If Philoumene's son Kallias had been home, I'd have had someone to talk to. But he was eighteen now, so he was at school, practicing horse-riding and sword-fighting and reciting Homer, and all the other things that girls can never learn.

After half an hour, I was so bored that I *almost* asked if I could help with the spinning. But Eirene's eyes were red and puffy, and Geta's face was grim. It seemed tactless to interrupt, even to offer help.

A door slammed in the women's quarters upstairs, and the mood in the courtyard shifted. I felt, as much as saw, Geta and Eirene stiffen. They kept their faces blank, but their bodies were alert, like sheep that smelled a wolf. Philoumene kept talking to my mother, but her shoulders rose a little way towards her ears.

What horror was about to descend on us? A many-headed serpent? A gorgon? I looked up to the verandah.

It was worse than a gorgon. Philoumene's mother-in-law Cleo stood at the top of the stairs in another new dress of fine purple wool edged with navy meander patterns. She posed like a foreign queen come to visit Athens. Her hair was ornately braided and pinned behind her head, with a delicate silver net adorning the careful work of art, and her throat was circled with gold and masses of softly-glowing pearls.

Who would she bad-mouth first?

Cleo paraded down the wooden stairs to the courtyard. She'd moved in with her oldest son, Philoumene's husband, after her own husband died in mid-winter. She kissed my mother, smiling regally, but totally ignored me, as usual.

She turned imperiously to Philoumene. "I need that lazy young slave to help me in the kitchen," she said, gesturing at Eirene. "You can spare her from the spinning, I assume." She looked down her nose and added, "The thread looks lumpy anyway."

Just for the record, she was wrong. The thread was far smoother and finer than I could ever have managed. But no one was asking me.

Philoumene's normally cheery voice had the edge of someone working hard to sound calm. "Very well. Eirene, go and help my mother-in-law in the kitchen as she asked. Can you wait here in the courtyard for us, Apollonia? I'll pop upstairs and finish getting ready, then I'll go to the agora with you and your mother. Demetria, old friend, you come with me to keep me company. Geta, you will help me dress. Leave the baby down here. And Apollonia, could you please keep an eye on him?"

I tried to smile politely. At this rate, we would *never* get to the agora, or my earrings. My mother and her friend dawdled up the wooden stairs, still talking a thousand words a minute, followed by old Geta. Young Eirene dragged herself to the kitchen door, where Philoumene's mother-in-law stood, glaring, with her hands on her hips.

"Hurry up, girl!" Cleo barked. "I want you to roast these almonds, then grind them very fine. Now, not next month!"

Eirene was only a bit older than me. She and her friends had been gathering ripe plums from a grove of wild trees close to their village in Scythia when the slavers had surrounded them, killed one boy who tried to fight, and put them all in chains. She'd been bought and resold at slave markets all around the Mediterranean until she'd ended up here.

My father once told me that whether you were citizen or slave, free or captive, was the will of the gods. Some people were fit to be free, and some were more fit to be slaves. But it didn't seem a very good answer to me. What if a slaver captured *me*, Apollonia, in the agora today, or on our farm? Would that mean that the gods suddenly decided *I* was more fit to be a slave?

"Useless girl!" Cleo shouted at Eirene. "I told you *not* to roast the almonds before you ground them. Now the whole batch is ruined. What a waste! You will have to start again from scratch. My son was a fool to buy you. And don't give me that sly look. I've never trusted you. If I had my way, you'd be down in the silver mines. You couldn't cause any trouble there."

I shivered at the thought, even in the warm sunlight. The silver mines down at Cape Sounion were the main source of our city's wealth—that was where the metal came from to make the famous coins with Athena's owl on one side. But no one lived long, working there in dust and fumes and filth. A strong man might last a few years before he fell and hurt himself, or caught pneumonia. Eirene wouldn't last a week.

Cleo kept shouting at the helpless slave girl. "Stop skulking in the corner. Come over here." A stick whistled through the air and thwacked on flesh once, twice, three times.

All was quiet, then, except for quiet sobs from the kitchen and the thudding of a pestle on nuts in a mortar.

Then things got worse. Cleo came to the kitchen doorway and glared at me. "You're a plain one, Apollonia. More like your father's side of the family than your mother's, though she's never made the most of what she's got. She doesn't look after herself like Philoumene does. No dress sense. She's obviously passed *that* on to you. And you've definitely got your father's nose. It doesn't look too bad on him. Pity about yours."

I just stared. Adults weren't supposed to say things like that. Not out loud, where you could hear them.

Cleo went on, "No wonder your father hasn't managed to marry you off yet. He'll have to hurry. You're already getting too old. Old and plain."

What?

Cleo spoke again: "If I could only teach Philoumene to take a firm enough hand with her slaves. My son and her, they're both far too soft. But she does take care of herself. I'll give her that." Cleo disappeared back into the kitchen to shout at Eirene again.

I didn't know whether I should laugh or cry. I wanted to talk to my mother, but she was still upstairs with Philoumene and Geta. Aphrodite's ankles, *how* could Philoumene possibly take so long getting dressed? The woman had been *almost* ready when we'd first turned up! Meanwhile, Eirene was a sobbing mess in the kitchen, and Cleo was more poisonous than a toad. The baby in the cradle was thankfully quiet, but otherwise no use at all.

Upstairs, Philoumene suddenly shrieked, "My jewelry! It's gone! My jewelry box is empty!"

Cleo ran out of the kitchen, dragging a sobbing Eirene. "It was her! The red-headed slave! I told you not to trust her. Look at that sly face!" She tied the girl's hands together with a long piece of rope—where had she got that from?—and gave a vicious yank. Eirene fell onto the hard surface of the courtyard, and lay there motionless.

Philoumene walked slowly down the stairs, clutching at the railing. Her face was white. "The box is still there, up in my room," she said quietly, "but everything's gone. Everything. What will my husband say?"

My mother and Geta followed close behind her. Philoumene was pale and breathing fast. Mother led her friend to the shaded side of the courtyard and sat her down, making soothing noises. "Bring me a fan, Geta."

"Gifts from my dead father," Philoumene cried. "Gifts from my husband. All gone. My mother's best necklace. My rings! My bangles! My earrings!"

Cleo gave her daughter-in-law a wide, satisfied smile that would curdle sheep's milk. "Don't call my son yet. Just wait. I'm sure I know where to look." She ran up the wooden stairs and rushed into the room that the female slaves shared. A moment later, she emerged onto the balcony with her hands full of gold and silver. "Well, look at this! Look what I found! It was under the red-headed slattern's pallet. Call for my son now. The thieving slave must be punished." She pranced down the stairs like a general who had won a great victory, her hands heaped with the spoils of war, and held the pile of finely-worked gold, silver and gems in front of her daughter-in-law.

Philoumene stared at the jewelry. "How did you know?"

Cleo smirked. "It was obvious."

Eirene sobbed more loudly.

Geta looked straight at me, as if she was trying to tell me something she didn't dare to say out loud.

The sun came out from behind a cloud, and odd patches of brightness flickered in the shady side of the courtyard, like shadows in reverse. It reminded me of an earlier time, half-remembered, when I saw something I'd never dared tell anyone about.

I looked up. The sun glinted on the golden wings of a griffin, flying high in the blue above the house, its eagle's beak open, its lion's body treading the air. It was real! So the griffins I remembered from my childhood *must* have been real. Now, as then, I knew that I could never tell the adults or I would be beaten for lying. Adults are hopeless at telling truth from lies.

All griffins loved gold; Herodotus told us so. Bright flashes reflected from the griffin's wings onto the mound of jewelry in Cleo's hands, and on the expensive-looking earring in Philoumene's left earlobe. A thought was tickling at the back of my mind. Gold ...

Only one earring, I suddenly realised. Philoumene was only wearing one earring, a luscious golden drop encrusted with fine granulations. Nothing in her right earlobe. Rings, but no bangles. No necklace. Something didn't add up.

"Philoumene," I said, "Geta was upstairs, helping you to dress, when Mother and I got here. Your hair was done, except for the circlet you usually wear around it. And had just one earring in, the one you're wearing now. Do you agree?"

"What are you talking about, child?" Philoumene put a hand to her left ear, then her right. "Oh. I suppose so. But I don't see what that has to do with all my jewelry being stolen out of the box."

I took a deep breath. "When Mother and I got here, you and Geta came down the stairs. Then we were all down here—all except Cleo. Then Cleo came downstairs and took Eirene away from her spinning and into the kitchen, and you and Mother and Geta went upstairs."

Flinging her hands out angrily, Philoumene said, "Yes, yes, but I still can't see what this can possibly have to do with my jewelry. How could I have been so stupid? Why did I trust that Skythian girl? What will my husband say?" She turned to my mother. "What should I do?"

I took another breath. "So, when we got here, Geta must have taken the earring you're wearing now out of your jewelry box and put it through your ear, and she would have been just about to get the other one out of the box. Then your bangles, and necklace, and the circlet. The box must have been full of jewelry then, or you both would have noticed."

Geta nodded, staring at me.

"Unless it was Geta who stole the jewelry, and planted it on the redhead," Cleo said brightly.

Geta lifted her eyes to the heavens.

I was quite sure, then, that I was right. "Just one more step, Philoumene. After you and Mother went back upstairs, Eirene was spinning in front of me, or working over there in the kitchen. She didn't go upstairs at all."

Cleo harrumphed like a camel. I wouldn't have been surprised if she spat like one.

"You're right, Apollonia." My mother looked startled.

Trembling slightly despite myself, I said, "The only person who could have taken the jewelry is the only one who was still upstairs after you came down to greet us, with Geta, and before you went back up."

Everyone looked at Cleo. There was a noise as if some fool had stepped on a lion's tail, then she screamed, "Yes, it was me! I took the jewelry and put it under the redhead's pallet, but it was for your own good, Philoumene. My son was a fool to buy her. She belongs in the silver mines, not here in a civilized house. She's worse than Pistos was, that scoundrel of a Thracian slave. Two thieving slaves in the same household! It's a good thing he's dead."

In a single moment, Philoumene went all the way from distraught to furious. She stepped over to Cleo. "That necklace you are wearing—I recognize the pearl at the centre, that egg-shaped pearl. It's the one I 'lost' years ago, when your son and I visited your house. You're a thief and a liar."

Cleo just opened and closed her mouth like a trout in clear water.

Geta went down on her creaky old knees in front of Philoumene. "Mistress, forgive me, I know this is forbidden, but I can't stay quiet any longer. Eirene saw Cleo smother Pistos when he was sleeping after the master beat him, and Cleo threatened to kill her if she said anything."

"The boy was robbing you blind," Cleo said, her voice cold. "You're better off without him. Or that treacherous old slave. She's no use to anyone."

My mother came to stand beside me. "Perhaps we should go, my dear."

"No, Demetria," her old friend said. "It's not you who should go. It's her." She glowered at her mother-in-law. "I want you packed and ready to leave within the hour. I will send word for my husband. One of his brothers can take you in. But I will warn them to watch you every moment. Hand me my jewelry now."

Cleo flung all Philoumene's rings and bracelets, earrings and necklaces, tiaras and hair ornaments across the courtyard. The treasure scattered like bright pebbles. "I was doing it to help you … you have no idea how to run a household … how do you expect to keep my son happy …"

Philoumene lifted poor sobbing Eirene by her elbows, and untied the rope that bound her hands. "I never believed half the things that woman said about you, Eirene, or about Pistos. I should have kept her away from you, and him. Geta, send one of the men to fetch my husband, and lock the street door. Then bring wine and cakes for everyone—except *her.*"

Mother and Philoumene settled into conversation in a sunny corner while Geta patted Eirene's shoulder and filled her cup. Everything was on the way to being fixed—but I was almost blinded by another golden flash from the griffin making another circuit of the sky above the house. Something was still wrong.

I walked over to question Geta. She knew more about the family than anyone. And there had been another suspicious death in the family.

"Cleo's husband," I said. "No one told me what he died of, just that it was sudden. Not suitable information for a girl my age, I suppose. And Cleo doesn't look much like a grieving widow."

Geta sighed. "Slaves talk to slaves. He went to bed one night looking fine, then the vomiting and diarrhea started. He was dead by morning. Cleo insisted that it was dysentery caused by overindulgence. But he was never fat."

"Poison?"

"Yes," Geta said, flatly. "The cook saw Cleo buy poison for mice in the storeroom. But there were no mice."

It was obvious. "So she could come to live here with her eldest son in luxury. She just had to get rid of the slaves she didn't like so everything would be perfect."

"And no one would believe us slaves. No one ever does."

"I believe you, Geta. But I won't report Cleo to the magistrates." I couldn't do that to Geta. The magistrates weren't allowed to hear evidence from a slave unless it was taken under torture.

Geta nodded. She knew that.

"Cleo's always been horrible to me," I said.

"You're smarter than she is," Geta said. "She hates that!"

The griffin circled the sky again, shining like a small sun, then flew off to the north. I gazed after it. Perhaps one day ...

"All right, wife, you've convinced me. Son, would you please fetch your grandmother's boxes down from upstairs?"

Tall Kallias, Philoumene's eldest, climbed the stairs again and again to bring Cleo's many boxes of possessions down to the courtyard, then helped his father to search them. I wasn't surprised when they found a number of small, precious items that had accidentally fallen into the boxes and hidden themselves inside Cleo's dresses and cloaks. Each time Kallias found one, he held it up for me to see. When he unearthed a particularly sweet silver cup in the shape of a hedgehog, he winked at me when no one was looking. Once the search was finished, Kallias and his father marched Cleo out of the house.

Perhaps Cleo's words were not all lies. Perhaps neither Mother nor I had any dress sense. Perhaps I really was too old and plain, at sixteen, for Father to find me a husband. But even that might not be true. Kallias didn't think I was too plain to wink at. And, unlike his grandmother, I didn't steal my relatives' jewelry, or murder people.

I was sure, now, that I really must have seen griffins when I was younger, as I did again today. Even the much-travelled Herodotus couldn't say that.

Hours later, my mother and I finally reached the agora. The fishmongers were sold out of tuna and even of sardines, but there were spicy Spartan-style sausages at the butchers, and perky green asparagus and leeks at the vegetable stall, and fat dates from Syria.

Best of all, though, the griffin earrings that I'd longed for still sat gleaming in the middle of the goldsmith's display. Soon they glittered in my ears like tiny suns.

FOR A BETTER CITY

Peter W. J. Hayes

Live in the moment, the counselors in rehab told him. The way they explained it, Charlie always thought they meant slow down, forget the past and the future. Burrow into your here and now. He gave it a try, feeling vaguely silly. But he couldn't dismiss the pedestrians as they hurried past the coffee shop's front window. The panel trucks and black Town Cars idling in traffic. He flinched at a hissing sound and caught himself. Just steam from a frothing wand.

He didn't like the "live in the moment" phrase. He preferred the idea of "centering," as explained to him by Jeb, who ran the half-way house where he stayed. Charlie translated it as staying true to himself, without ignoring everything around him. That fit with his situational awareness training in the Army, before his return home and the headlong pitch into booze.

He breathed in slowly. Whichever worked. He guessed today he would need all the help he could find.

Right on time, Ivan pushed through the front door and stopped, his pale eyes scanning the tables. He acknowledged Charlie with an upward flick of his chin and signaled toward the barista. Charlie returned the nod and watched Ivan's shoulders swing to match each stride as he walked to the counter. The movement gave him a feral, aggressive quality, like a big cat advancing on prey. The young barista shrank into herself as he approached, and Charlie knew she'd seen it too.

Charlie let out his breath. When Ivan invited him to the coffee shop, he'd considered not showing up, but there were things he couldn't reconcile. One was why Ivan—who didn't live in the half-way house—was allowed in whenever he wanted. But most of all, it was the way Ivan's kindness to residents evaporated if he thought no one was watching. In those moments, Charlie had seen Ivan's gaze turn hard and calculating, as if he was assigning each person a value, defining them as a variable he might need later to solve an equation. Eight months ago, Charlie wouldn't have cared. For some reason, now he did. He guessed it had something to do with his six months of sobriety, with needing to know if he could still handle himself in a tight spot.

So he'd decided to show up. Play it out.

Ivan placed his coffee on the table and sat in the chair across from him. "Charlie. You doing well? Hanging in there?" It was the easy, open-faced Ivan, the man of relaxed smiles and quick jokes. The one who remained non-judgmental about Charlie's arrests and court-ordered rehab.

"Working on it," Charlie said, noncommittally. The universal answer of everyone in the half-way house. He'd seen people shift their inflection to fit their mood, signaling commitment, irony, or defeat.

Ivan's pale eyes turned frank, his brow wrinkled in concern. "I worry about you, you know. I'm rooting for you. I want you to make it out of Jeb's place." Ivan tried his coffee and placed it back on the table. "I was thinking about what might hold you back. Stop you getting out as soon as you can."

"Uh-huh."

"I mean, look around." Ivan swept his hand toward the window and looked outside. "All those people out there. Be good if you were with them." His pale eyes turned hard, the same look Charlie had seen in the half-way house when Ivan thought no one was watching.

Charlie followed Ivan's gaze. Hanging from a building across the street was a banner proclaiming Arthur Horstop's city council win. The photo showed a confident black man, round-faced, a red silk tie hanging from a perfectly tailored collar. Charlie saw confidence in Arthur's eyes, and from the set of his mouth, certainty. He was a reformer. Below the photo was the phrase, 'For a better city,' and Charlie was certain Arthur believed that. He turned back to the table.

Ivan's eyes were still hard. Charlie remembered the scuttlebutt that Ivan was connected the mob. "You glad Horstop won?" he asked, guessing at the answer.

Ivan blinked and turned back to him, the friendliness reappearing on his face as if someone had thrown a switch. "The guy we had was good. This guy is more complicated."

Despite Ivan's smile and light tone, Charlie heard barely hidden disgust and noted the word 'we.' He remembered the bribery scandal that sunk the incumbent, leading to Arthur's win.

More math that wasn't hard to do.

"Anyway," Ivan said, giving his paper coffee cup a quarter turn. "I think we have a solution for that. But I was talking about *you*. Listen, Charlie. You're a good guy, I can see that, and I want to help you out. Did you find a job yet?"

"Working on it. I don't need much."

"You need enough to live. And you aren't getting paid for the job Jeb gave you. Which is bullshit. I told him that."

Charlie shrugged. He was now the half-way house's medical first responder. Jeb made the decision soon after Charlie's arrival, after Jeb hesitated beside a comatose resident in the common room. Charlie—a combat medic with two tours in Afghanistan—recognized the symptoms of an overdose, grabbed the Narcan injector from Jeb's medical bag and rammed it into the man's thigh. And Ivan was right. Jeb said nothing about paying him, but in truth Charlie hadn't asked.

"I'll work it out," Charlie answered. "And I don't mind being on call."

"Well," Ivan's eyes slid to one side, as if he was considering options. He reached into his pocket and placed a flip phone on the table. "I bought you this. I figured you don't have a phone. It's a prepay, it's got ten hours on it. It'll help with your job search. You need your own number, those house phones are terrible."

Charlie stared at the phone. This was the start. Little things. Stuff almost impossible to refuse.

"It won't bite." Ivan laughed lightly and slid it halfway across the table. "Use it as much as you want. I just have one request. Keep one hour on it. In case I need to call you."

Charlie met his gaze. "Why would you need to call me?"

"Look, we're friends. And I have a favor to ask. I'm hoping you can help me out. I may call because of that."

They stared at one another, silent. Charlie had expected this. He knew Ivan asked people at the halfway house to do small jobs for him sometimes. Pick up a car, drive it somewhere and leave it. Watch someone's movements for a few hours. He paid well. And Charlie guessed that his own value to Ivan might be higher than the others. He knew how to treat gunshot wounds and trauma, and he suspected that someone in Ivan's line of work would find that useful. Especially if it avoided a trip to the hospital.

Charlie felt himself centering, focusing. He knew Ivan was sizing him up. From the corner of his eye, he saw the barista give them a furtive glance. He was aware of people trailing past the window. He decided to see this through. "What favor?" he asked softly.

Ivan reached into the pocket of his bomber jacket, produced a brown paper bag and gently placed it on the table. Slid it past the phone to him. "Take a look, but keep it in the bag. Just look."

Charlie unrolled the top and separated the sides. Inside he saw brushed nickel, the black hand grip of a revolver. He rolled up the bag. "What exactly do you want me to do with this?"

"Just hold it for me. I'll call you when I need it. Four days, maybe five. That's all."

"I get caught with this on probation and I'm back in the can. For a lot longer. You know I can't take this."

Ivan opened his hands, palms up. "It's only a few days. And the higher the risk the higher the reward. I know you need money. A thousand dollars now, another thousand when you deliver it to me."

Charlie watched Ivan's face. He showed no nervousness, he almost seemed to be in his zone. Confident. He knows I'll take it, Charlie thought. I'm like all the other guys in that house. Broke. Dying to be involved in something. Bored out of our minds and desperate to fill the damn hole where the drunkenness or drugs once lived. Wanting a way to keep Ivan at least acting as if he was his friend.

Charlie reached across the table, picked up the phone and slid it into his jeans. He met Ivan's gaze. "So. Where's the thousand bucks?"

Charlie lay in his bed staring at the ceiling, listening to the sounds of the half-way house. Institution buildings, he thought, never sleep. Even now, near midnight, heating pipes gurgled and clunked, a distant door slammed. Despite the curfew, he made out the voices of two people talking. Even when all the noises disappeared, the silence was poised, waiting.

He looked at the phone Ivan had given him. It sat on the empty desk next to the lamp, attached to its charging wire. He knew what he had to do. In Texas it would be almost ten o'clock. He hesitated.

For the hundredth time he thought of the handgun, but no new ideas surfaced. Perhaps it was used in a crime, perhaps not. Perhaps it was intended for a crime, perhaps not. He was being tested, he knew for a fact, but tested how? He'd found a place for it in the basement, duct-taped to the top of a ventilation run. A police search would find it, but with a little luck they wouldn't connect it to him. He did know two things for sure. It was a Smith and Wesson .38 with an enclosed hammer, a small revolver designed for concealment. And given the smell of oil, its last owner cared for the weapon.

He rolled onto his side and stared at the phone. Finally, in a single motion, he raised himself to a sitting position, unplugged it and dialed a number from memory.

The response followed the third ring. "Hello?" Charlie heard the West Texas drawl that extended the word, the sweetness of the young woman's voice.

A wave of guilt and sadness rose inside him. "Hey Amy," he said, pushing it away. "It's Charlie."

"Charlie." The way she spoke felt like a hug. "You're out of prison?"

"I am. I'm in a half-way house. Six months here. Unless I can find a job, then I'm out sooner."

"Uh huh." The loudest silence Charlie had ever heard floated between them. "You sound good. Are you good?"

She meant sober. She's worried I'm drunk, he thought. Whether this call was going to be me blubbering and crying. Or angry. He lifted his legs and lay flat on the bed, staring at the gloomy ceiling. "Six months sober. I feel good."

"I'm glad, Charlie." A lilt lifted her voice.

"Tell me what you're up to."

"I've got one semester left in nursing school. I'm real close. It's starting to get real."

"Good. You're gonna be great." He squinted at the ceiling. "How's Jeff doing?"

Another long pause. "Same old same old. You know how it is."

He did. In a rush he remembered that smell as he clambered over the bomb crater to Jeff's Humvee. He shrank from the memory. "Hey. They made me the first responder here in the half-way house. I'm back into medicine. I have a walkie-talkie in case they need me. I've been building out their med kit. Bought some first aid stuff, scrounged some other things. Found a messenger bag to carry everything. I'm pretty much set." Ivan's money had helped him at the local drugstore. The scrounging part was trickier. They'd had two more overdoses in the last few weeks. When the paramedics were focused on the patient, he'd lifted some drugs from their supplies. Epinephrin. Ketamine. Pain killers. He knew they would come up missing when they inventoried, but so far no one had come asking.

"That's good, Charlie. Maybe you could get back into it. Become a paramedic or something?"

"Maybe." He knew there was no chance, given his prison record. "But tell me about nursing school. Taking care of Jeff has to help you there."

"Oh yeah." She laughed, light and happy. "I've been helping him for so long I already know half the stuff in my classes. My teachers keep saying I ask the smartest questions. It's just because when I read the textbook, sometimes I know it doesn't work the way they say. And I've done real well on my practicals. Same thing. I've done so much of the stuff I'm not nervous."

The sweetness of her voice ached inside him. "And now you can get paid for it."

"Maybe. That'll take a while. I have to pay back my school loans. Jeff's Mom has been real good. She comes over to help out. That's how I was able to do my practicals. She covered for me."

"Good."

The silence ebbed between them. Charlie ran his palm over his face. "Okay, I should go. Just wanted to check in." He hesitated. "Tell Jeff I said hello."

A trickle of breath. "Charlie, I'm sorry, I don't think I can do that."

Charlie blinked into the gloom.

"I don't mean to be difficult." Her voice was still sweet, the gentleness unaffected, but something stone-hard was there. "He gets so agitated if I mention you. It goes on for a day or two. He fights me on everything. Takes swings at me." She paused. "I'm just being honest."

Charlie stayed silent. He closed his eyes and tried to focus, to center himself.

"Charlie?"

He opened his eyes. "Yes?"

A momentary hitch, then, "What happened, Charlie? That day? Did something happen I don't know about? I know you and Jeff were good friends, and you're the only one from your unit who still calls, but I don't understand."

The blood in his veins turned barbed and sluggish. Somewhere in the building someone shouted, the sound echoing through the hallways. Reflexively, Charlie glanced at the walkie-talkie. It remained silent. He turned his gaze to the ceiling. Closed and opened his eyes. An ocean of booze hadn't diluted or killed this feeling. It never would.

He should tell her. She'd been honest with him, it was his turn. She deserved it. He was the one who did this to her, after all. To Jeff's mother as well. He remembered Jeff showing him Amy's photo, from their honeymoon just six months before he deployed. She was barely twenty-one. In the photo she was standing on a hill-top in high grass. A straw cowboy hat was pulled tight to her gold aviator sunglasses. The wind streamed her light brown hair from her head and flattened her sundress against her stomach and thighs. She was smiling, happy. A photo that radiated beauty and lightness.

He had ended all that.

"There's," he started and stopped. It was too much. He closed his eyes and spoke not to the photo, but to the darkness of his eyelids. "After the blast, when I got to Jeff, it was bad." That image conjured itself against his eyelids. The Humvee on its side, Jeff sitting against it, staring down at the stumps of his legs. The red slash than from his lower abdomen into his groin. His hands hovering at waist level, as if he wasn't sure what to do first. "I got a tourniquet around his first leg. I was starting on the second." He breathed. "You have to understand, something like that, most people are knocked out by the blast. Or in shock. But Jeff was lucid." He hesitated, the thickness of his blood slowing his tongue. "He told me to stop. He told me not to do it, not to send him back to you like that. He told me to take off the tourniquet. Let him bleed out. He made me promise I would."

Through the phone Amy's breath was a sunlit summer stream over smooth-rounded rocks.

Charlie licked his lips. "Then he lost consciousness."

"And you saved him."

Charlie shuddered. "They drilled it into us. Keep the casualty numbers down. Save everyone. It's all they cared about. So yeah. I applied the other tourniquet, QuikClot the belly wound. Prepped him for transport."

"You kept him alive. After you promised."

Charlie opened his mouth to speak but nothing came out. He'd obeyed his commanders, put his skills to work. But he hadn't saved anyone, he'd imprisoned them. Jeff in his own body, Amy to caring for him. Jeff's mother in the horror of what happened to her son. For how long? How long?

"You did the right thing," Amy said through his phone, her words strained. "You're a good man. You don't have to carry that."

No, thought Charlie. She had to carry it. He'd treated the wounds, not the man. In doing that he'd stolen from Amy every pixel of beauty in that photo. He'd betrayed both her and Jeff, and there wasn't enough booze in the world to put that right.

He knew that now.

"I'm sorry," he managed to say, and disconnected the call.

Two nights later, ninety minutes before curfew, the flip phone rang. Charlie, hunched over his desk reading a magazine article on Buddhism, jerked upright.

The screen listed the caller as unknown, but Charlie knew it was Ivan. He pressed the accept button and mumbled 'hello.'

"Charlie," a ragged breath. "I need a favor." A long pause and Charlie heard a soft whistle. He knew the sound. Something was wrong with Ivan's nose.

"Do you want the package you gave me?"

"No." Another rustling breath, the gentle whistle. "Leave it there. I'll text you an address. Just get here. Soon as you can. Bring your med kit."

The address, when it arrived on his phone, was five blocks away. A few minutes later Charlie signed out of the half-way house with a joke about going to a diner, the brown paper bag with the revolver nestled among his medical supplies.

He walked to the address, the messenger bag nudging his hip with each step. Along the way, the row houses gradually improved in appearance, the crumbling cement steps transformed into sharp-edged ones with railings and flower pots. The dented metal screen doors evolved into wooden doors gleaming with paint. He found the address on a street lined with shiny late-model cars. He knocked lightly and the door yawned open. He stepped into an entry, and using his elbow, pushed the door closed behind him.

The room to his left was dark. "Up here." Ivan stood at the top of the wide stairway. The front of Ivan's white shirt was soaked with blood. He held a small towel under his nose.

Charlie climbed to him. As he took the last step Ivan dropped the towel, grabbed a handful of Charlie's shirt, swung him around and slammed him up against the wall. Reflexively, Charlie grabbed Ivan's wrists, causing Ivan to pull him from the wall and jam him back against it.

"You and I need to understand each other," Ivan hissed, his face a few inches from Charlie's. "You're in this now. I'll make it worth your while, but you need to keep quiet. One screw up and I will turn your life to shit. Guaranteed."

Charlie thought of the revolver. He understood, finally. It was leverage. All Ivan had to do was drop an anonymous call to his parole officer saying he'd seen Charlie with it. Describe it. A quick search of the halfway-house and back to jail he would go.

Anger and fear roiled inside him.

But he'd promised himself to play this out. He was sick of Ivan using the half-way house to groom people. Recruit them. Through clenched lips, he asked, "How much worth my while?"

Ivan's pale eyes didn't shift. "Double what I promised for the gun."

"Paid tonight?"

"Tonight."

They stared at one another. Charlie let go of Ivan's wrists and Ivan unclenched Charlie's shirt. A drop of blood dripped from Ivan's nose. Ivan scooped up the towel.

"You need to take care of that," Charlie said with a small smile.

Ivan pressed the towel back to his nose and pointed through a wide arch into another room.

Inside, Charlie found a living room and a young man face down on a thick oriental rug. All he wore was underwear. An upended chair lay nearby. Charlie kneeled and saw a bloody indentation on the back of the man's head. He tugged on latex gloves and checked for a pulse. Nothing. The math wasn't hard to do.

He looked at Ivan. "He's dead."

"He's not the problem. He is." Ivan nodded farther into the room, toward the back of the house. A single lamp showed a pair of loafer-clad feet protruding from the shadows at the end of a couch. Charlie rose. He found a black man sitting with his back to the wall, chin on his chest, breathing in shallow rasps. His shirt was unbuttoned and partially pulled out of his pants. Charlie kneeled in front of him. He knew him. It was Arthur Horstop, newly elected member of City Council.

A quick flash of his pencil light into Arthur's eyes told him Arthur was drugged. His pulse was thready but regular. Charlie stood up. "How is he the problem?"

Ivan waved a hand at him. "He can't be found here."

"He's drugged. Give it time and he'll walk out."

"Yeah. Sure. *Now* he's too drugged to do anything." Ivan's sarcasm was tinged with anger.

Charlie took in the underwear-clad dead man, the pair of highball glasses on the coffee table. One lay on its side in the middle of a puddle. He didn't have all the variables, but he had enough to understand this was a zero-sum game, not algebra.

"What was he drugged with?" Charlie asked.

Ivan looked at the coffee table. "Roofie."

"Rohypnol?"

"Yeah. But he didn't drink enough. Or he got wise. It looked like he was sliding off so we started to undress him for some photos. He started swinging. Stevie caught the edge of the table with his head. Arthur got in a good punch before I dropped him."

"Broke your nose."

"Tell me about it." He adjusted the towel under his nose. "You need to get him out of here. His car is parked outside. Just take him somewhere and leave him at the wheel."

Charlie glanced at Arthur. His fingers were twitching as if he was playing piano in a dream. "I don't get it," Charlie said quietly. "Why don't you just leave, call the cops. They see this and Arthur's done. That's what you want, right? Get rid of him for a guy you can work with?" Charlie knew he was asking too many questions, but he needed to know.

Ivan stared at him. "I can't have him telling the cops about Stevie and me. Better to have him wake up someplace, remember this but think he got away clean." He held up his phone. "Then I show up with photos of him next to Stevie's body. Threaten to tell the cops. That works as good as the photos we were going to take. Not great, but we'll have him. So I need him out of here."

Charlie thought about it. For everything Ivan did wrong, he was smart. He had to match that. He considered the mechanics. "How far is his car from the front door?"

Ivan relaxed. "Right outside."

"Okay." He looked at Arthur, who raised his head for a few seconds and dropped it again. "He's getting close to where he just needs help to walk. I'll get him downstairs. You need to follow us in your car so I can get a ride back." He held out his hand. "Money."

Ivan pursed his lips, but slid a hand into his pants pocket. From a wad of bills he counted out two thousand dollars. Charlie dropped the bills into his messenger bag.

"Go get your car," Charlie said quickly.

Ivan tried to smile but it seemed to hurt. "You and I are going to get along." He turned for the stairs.

Charlie let him take a few steps and called after him. "Wait. I should give you something for your nose. Especially if you have to drive."

Ivan stopped and turned back to him. "Like what?"

"Some pain relief and a boost so you can focus. I'll try and set your nose later. Roll up your sleeve."

Ivan hesitated, but did what he was asked. Charlie filled a syringe, and before Ivan could change his mind, gave him a quick stab in the arm. "Okay." He turned back to Arthur, focused on how to get him upright as he watched Ivan from the corner of his eye.

As Ivan reached the arched doorway he staggered. Charlie walked up behind him. Ivan pushed away from the wall and veered toward the stairway. "What?" he mumbled, grabbing for the banister.

He never touched it.

Charlie's push between the shoulder blades pitched Ivan face-first down the stairs, leaving a streak of blood on the white carpet of the last four steps. Charlie followed him down. Ivan lay murmuring to himself, his body rigid. Charlie went through Ivan's pockets and removed his money and phone. Careful not to touch it, he slid the revolver from its brown bag and positioned it next to Ivan's hand.

He leaned over Ivan. "I gave you Ketamine, asshole. Special K. Same as a roofie. But this time the K stands for karma."

It took some work, but five minutes later Charlie was driving Arthur's car, Arthur asleep in the passenger seat.

Charlie and Arthur were sitting at Arthur's kitchen table when dawn broke. After finding Arthur's home address on the insurance card in the car's glove box, Charlie only stopped long enough to make an anonymous 911 call about Stevie's body, then dump the empty Ketamine vial and syringe, brown paper bag, and phones down a storm drain. Arthur's wife, it turned out, was out of town, which made things easier.

When Arthur woke he was skeptical Charlie was helping him, until Charlie held up a plastic bag with the two glasses from Stevie's coffee table.

"Did you leave your fingerprints anywhere else?"

Slowly, as Arthur recovered, they reconstructed Ivan's plan. Stevie was a plant who'd worked in Arthur's campaign. His story of a rich father wanting to contribute to Arthur's next campaign the ruse to get Arthur into the house.

Arthur swigged from his third bottle of water, still working hard to flush his system. "Stevie told me his dad wanted to meet me, man to man. Just us three."

"And that didn't sound right to you?" Charlie asked.

"No. Those big contributors, they want people around. Helps them feel like big shots. That was why I was careful drinking. It didn't feel right to me."

"I guess the idea was to get some photos of you half undressed with Stevie. Threaten to make them public. They wanted leverage."

They fell silent. Charlie was tired, and he knew Arthur had to be exhausted. "I should go," Charlie said.

"Where to?"

"I can't go back to the half-way house. When the cops put the screws to Ivan he'll name me. I'll be back in jail before I can tie my shoes. I don't know. As far from here as I can get."

Arthur nodded slowly. "I wish there was something I could do."

"Believe it or not, you already have." Charlie rose.

Arthur stood and they shook hands.

Charlie could see Arthur wanted to ask something. "If you've got something to say ..."

"Yeah. Why'd you do it? You could have walked. Or done what Ivan wanted."

Charlie thought about that. "You know," he said softly, "my last name is Krill. Until maybe sixth grade I always liked it. Then I found out what krill really is. Food for whales. Krill spend their lives waiting to be eaten. I guess that's it. I'm tired of being whale food. The army, connected guys like Ivan. The Goddam prison system. All the things people want you to do. The ways you blame yourself for stuff. We're just food in an ocean of whales. Hiding doesn't work. I know that now. But I won't be food, not anymore."

Arthur smiled, his brown eyes deep. "You and I could get along."

"Maybe," Charlie said, an image rising in front of him of Jeff trapped in his bed, Amy adjusting his IV and pillows. "But only if we can figure out a way to get along with ourselves, first."

THE DEVIL IN SISTER JONES

Beth Andrews

When Pastor Jones died, the whole settlement just about went crazy. So much had happened in the months before his death, this was like the final blow that nobody ever could have expected. People say they don't believe in the Devil, but I tell you he's just as real as you and me. I know what I know, and I know what I saw with my own two eyes.

It was over sixty years ago now, when I lived on the Family Islands in Sea Grape Bay. Back then I used to go to the First Apostolic Church of the Word of the Lord, Limited. Our old pastor, Reverend Rolle, had died of a heart attack. Well, he was over ninety with one foot in the grave and the other had no business anywhere else. After he was buried, they sent away for a new minister. After a couple of months while the elders and deacons tried to run the church, Pastor Jones came down from somewhere up North: Florida or Miami, or someplace like that.

Reverend Jones was one of them good old fire-and-brimstone preachers. The first Sunday he preached, three sisters got full of the Spirit and two more fell out in church! He was about fifty and his head was bald as a brass bed knob. But he was a godly man—a real saint. I never heard anybody speak a bad word about him.

Reverend Jones had a wife who came with him too. She was at least twenty years younger than him and she looked like some kind of Hollywood star or something. Man, that woman was a beauty! But she was active in community work. She led a Bible study, started a sewing circle and all that kind of thing.

It was nearly a year after they arrived that the trouble started.

Reverend and Mrs. Jones was sitting at home one Saturday night when Brother Bill come by to see them. Now Brother Bill was a pretty new member of the flock. He was a big, handsome fella from Long Island with olive skin and slick black hair. One time he was a real Hell-cat, drinking and romancing everything in a skirt. But after he met Pastor Jones and his wife, Bill started going to church real regular. One night he took off speaking in tongues, and before you know it he was saved, baptized and sanctified too. Now he was singing in the choir, studying the scriptures and collecting the offering after the service. He was best friends with Reverend Jones and his misses.

Anyhow, this night he come by and said, "Brother Jones, I hear that poor Sister Berthamae done took a turn for the worst. The sip-sip is that she won't last till the morning."

The minister jumped up and said he had better go see Sister Bertha before it was too late. Mind you, Sister Bertha was one of those who is always knocking at Death's door every week but manages to turn back before they cross his threshold. Still, Reverend Jones was real concerned, so he told Brother Bill to stay and keep company with Sister Jones. Then he ran out faster than a cat with its tail on fire.

Now in those days the preachers didn't have no fancy cars and big houses like today. Reverend Jones only had one old bicycle, so he hopped on and rode off. Berthamae lived in the next settlement, so it would take him more than an hour on foot.

Well, he was making good time but he hadn't gone very far when he got by the shore and saw one man coming up out of the bush with a basket full of fish. The man could see the moonlight reflecting off Rev's bald head, and he sang out loudly,

"Evenin' Rev! Where you going in such a hurry?"

Brother Jones had already passed him by now, but he stopped quick and turned around. He was real surprised, because the fisherman was Sister Bertha's son, Zeke.

"What you doing out fishing, Zeke?" Reverend Jones demanded, "Don't you care that your poor old mother is so sick?"

"Who say so?" Zeke asked, just as surprised as the preacher.

"Brother Bill just told me all about it."

"Brother Bill must be mix-up," Zeke answered him. "My ma was doing just fine when I left her this evening. I think somebody was pulling he leg!"

It took quite a while for Zeke to convince him, but finally the older man took his bike and headed back home. He wasn't gone more than half an hour, so he was kind of bewildered again when he stepped in the front door and didn't see any sign of either Sister Jones or Brother Bill. Not only was the porch empty, but the sitting room was deserted too.

Then he heard a noise that sounded like it was coming from the bedroom, so he stepped forward to investigate. When he reached the bedroom door, he heard a moaning and groaning coming from the other side and a screeching and scrunching sound like the old bed was going to bust all the springs. He felt like the whole house was shaking.

He lifted his hand to push the door open, but the latch was on inside. Then he heard Brother Bill beyond the wood, as plain as day:

"You want it, Sister Jones? You want it?"

"Yes! Oh yes, I want it!" This was the voice of his wife. "I got to have it, Bill! Oooooh!"

There was more moaning and shaking and screeching till Reverend Jones couldn't hold back any longer. He found his own voice at last, calling out, "What's going on in there? Are you all right, Sister Jones?"

Dead silence. Everything stopped at once. Reverend Jones didn't know what to do, so he started to pray.

"Lord deliver us!" he cried out. "There's something evil in this house! The Devil is here: I can feel it. But I'm ready to do battle with you, Satan. Come out and show yourself, you wicked demon."

When he finished speaking, the latch clicked, the bedroom door swung open with a loud squeak, and Brother Bill stumbled out, mopping his brow with his handkerchief. He was sweating and panting, and his shirt was half unbuttoned, revealing a well-muscled chest.

"What's happening, Brother Bill?" the preacher asked him. "Where's my wife?"

"She's right behind me, Brother Jones," Bill said. "But I think we'd best go in the sitting room. I got some serious news for you."

By now Reverend Jones was so excited and confused that he didn't know where he was anyway, so he went with the other man into the little sitting room. A couple of minutes later, Sister Jones joined them, looking real flushed and with her clothes all wrinkled and torn. The three of them sat down together and Brother Bill started to tell his tale.

"As God is my witness, Rev," he said, shaking his head as if he could hardly believe it himself, "you wasn't gone five minutes when your wife started to talk out of her head. She was shaking and carrying on so that I had to grab hold of her and put my arms around her tight-tight. Then she got away and ran into the bedroom. She was tearing off her dress and everything—and if I didn't throw her down on the bed and jump on top of her to hold her down, I don't know what would have happened next!"

Poor Reverend Jones almost turned green.

"You know what this is, don't you?" He put his face in his hands for a moment before looking back up at the other two. "This is a clear case of Devil Possession! An evil spirit done got hold of my poor wife."

He went to sit beside her and held her close to him while she started to weep softly into his shoulder.

"But what," Reverend Jones asked suddenly, "was you asking her if she wanted, Brother Bill? I could hear you through the door."

"Well," Bill stammered, hesitating a moment, "I know what Sister Jones needed and I told her she only had to say the word and she would have peace that passeth understanding. Peace like a river—"

"And joy like a fountain!" Mrs. Jones finished for him. "And Brother Bill sure gave it to me."

"God bless you, Brother Bill," Reverend Jones exclaimed, wiping a tear from his eye. "The Lord sent you here tonight to sustain my wife in her hour of need. I don't know what she would have done without you."

"Any man would have done the same!" Bill protested, reddening.

"Ah!" the minister said, "But not every man got what you got."

"That's the truth," Sister Jones agreed. "I tell you, husband, I had something inside of me tonight like I never felt before. I can never thank Brother Bill enough for what he did to—I mean for me."

So Brother Bill went home with words of praise ringing in his ears. For a couple of days, it looked like everything was back to normal. Then, a few nights later, after supper, Sister Jones's eyes started to roll up in her head and she fell on the floor in a fit—quaking and shaking something awful! When she got some control back, she began to shout.

"Call Brother Bill!" she cried loudly. "Send for Brother Bill. It ain't nobody else could save me now."

So Reverend Jones ran out into the street to fetch the good brother from his little house only a few hundred yards away.

"You got to come quick," he said, panting. "You got to minister to my wife. You got the gift of healing and she say nothing but your hands could do her any good."

"I'll be happy to lay hands on Sister Jones," Brother Bill answered readily. He went behind the minister right away.

"I only hope she's all right," Pastor Jones said.

"This is one powerful spirit, Brother Jones," the younger man responded, choosing his words carefully. "I almost believe it's Satan himself. I'll do whatever I can, but it's going to take plenty of prayer and fasting to do the job. And that's where you can help."

"Me?" The minister was eager but confused.

"We've got to divide the labor," Bill explained. "This is too much for one man. I'll take Sister Jones into the bedroom and do everything I can for her. Meantime, you got to take your Bible and walk from the dock to the lighthouse on the hill and back again seven times—because it took seven days to make the world and there's seven churches and seven hills in the book of Revelation. And all the time you're walking, you got to recite the twenty-third Psalm."

"So," Reverend Jones said slowly, "while I'm outside interceding with the Lord, you'll be inside with my wife, administering the laying on of hands."

"That's right." Brother Bill was pleased at his eagerness. "You do the praying and I'll do the laying!"

Reverend Jones did just what Brother Bill told him, and it took a long time because the dock and the lighthouse were almost a mile apart. But sure enough, when he got home around midnight, his wife was looking happier than ever.

But Satan wasn't done with Sister Jones yet—not by a long shot! After that, at least two or three times a week she used to have these spells—sometimes in broad daylight. Poor Brother Bill spent more time in the bedroom with her than he did in his own house; and people were dead tired of seeing Pastor Jones walking up and down the settlement, praying and reciting—and losing plenty of weight in the process.

Nobody could talk about anything else. There were prayer vigils and Bible chain readings at the church, and everybody was quoting scripture verses at each other non-stop. The only person in the settlement who didn't pay any mind to it was old Granny Jay. She told us we were all a bunch of fools who had two eyes (and some had four, if they wore glasses) and still couldn't see. When I told her the Devil had come amongst us, she sucked her teeth and said this was the first she knew the Devil was from Long Island. Her words didn't make any sense to me, so I left her alone after that.

Anyway, a few months went by and things weren't getting much better. Brother Jones was almost ready to call in a famous faith healer to deal with his wife's problems. Then one morning Sister Jones got up feeling sick and vomited up all her breakfast. At first nobody connected this with her condition, but after it happened a couple more times her husband was even more worried—especially when he noticed that her belly was starting to swell up too. But when he mentioned it to his wife, she almost had another fit.

"It's the Devil!" Sister Jones hollered. "The Devil done caused my belly to swell. Oh Lord, help me!"

Of course they had to send for Brother Bill again. He said it was no doubt that old serpent, Satan, was responsible for all the trials Sister Jones was going through.

But he had to be by himself to fast and pray before he could decide what was best to do about it. Well, it was just exactly three days and three nights when he came back to Reverend Jones, ready with his solution.

"Brother Jones," he declared, "I done had a vision. It was more like a dream. The Spirit has revealed to me that Satan is using your wife to get to you and destroy your ministry and all the work you're doing for the Lord."

By this time, Reverend Jones and everybody else figured that Brother Bill's word was Gospel: he had a direct line to Jesus. Nobody would doubt that whatever he said was true.

"What can I do, Bill?" Rev asked in desperation. "Tell me what to do!"

Brother Bill paused a moment before delivering his verdict.

"You've got to take your wife way out to sea in a dinghy and baptize her in salt water. That will fix Satan good."

"But I can't swim, Brother Bill!" Jones protested, staring at him.

"Fear not, brother," Bill reassured him. "The Lord is with you. But just in case, I'm going with you too."

The day of the baptism the whole town turned out to catch a glimpse of Rev, Sister Jones and Brother Bill when they set out early in the morning. We all watched the little boat, with Bill sculling, until it rounded Dead Man's Point. All day long we waited for them to return. Then, an hour or so before sunset, we saw the dinghy coming back to shore. But there were only two people in it: Brother Bill and Sister Jones. And what a story they had to report to us!

According to them, the two men were trying to lower Sister Jones into the water when the Devil flew into her for one final spree. She jumped about so much that the boat tipped over and all three fell overboard. Brother Bill struggled to get Sister Jones back into the boat, but when he turned to help the minister, a giant hand came up out of the water and pulled the older man down into the depths of the sea. Nobody ever saw him again.

Everybody was just heartbroken at the fate of poor Reverend Jones. Sister Jones was weeping and wailing and gnashing her teeth so much it was a pitiful sight. But one good thing: she never had one of those spells again, so I hear. Brother Bill's vision had to be true, even if it cost the preacher his life.

Sister Jones decided she was going back to America, and Brother Bill said it wasn't right for her to go alone—so he went with her. Somebody told me a few years after that Brother Bill married Sister Jones. They had five or six children, and started their own ministry somewhere near Atlanta. Well, after all he did for her, I guess it wasn't such a surprise.

Anyhow, now you know the story. It happened in my own settlement, and I was a witness, even though I was little more than a boy at the time. But I want you to tell me this: If that wasn't the work of the Devil, what was it?

IF AT FIRST YOU DON'T SUCCEED

Michael Mallory

Fortunately, Marie and the kids weren't at home when the package exploded. Bruce was, of course, and the blast that blew the garage door out propelled him back against the tool cabinet. Nobody would ever know how much pain he felt.

Police and fire trucks were there when the rest of the family returned. Robbie and Maddie, eight and six respectively, were prevented from going near the house despite their growing hysteria. Nobody wanted them to see what was left of their dad.

Practically all that remained of Bruce Finnerman was an inexplicable mystery: *who wanted to kill him with an explosive*?

Who wanted to kill him with *anything*?

Lou Beratti knew why he was being summoned by the big man, but since he also knew he had done nothing wrong, he wasn't worried.

He did the job he was hired to do and it was not his fault that it got screwed up. All he had to do was explain that.

He arrived at the penthouse suite of Western Towers on the Sunset Strip a little early, having used the private elevator that went straight to the top exclusively. At the appointed time Biggie Mann (that was really the name he used) emerged from his bathroom, which was rumored to contain a 14k gold toilet. On the way to his desk he grabbed a handful of grapes from a bowl and flicked one into the air, catching it with his mouth. Dropping into his oversized executive chair, still chewing, he asked, "See the news?"

"Biggie, I fulfilled my contract to the letter," Louie responded. "I was told to leave a bomb on the porch and I did."

"Yet the desired result was not achieved. The target, that Sowl woman, is still alive."

"I can't explain what happened. I don't know how the bomb made it to someone else's house. All I know is I dropped it at the address I was given."

Biggie Mann leaned forward and placed his beefy hands on his desk, and glared at Lou with cold basalt eyes. But Beratti refused to flinch and look away. He had no need to. He was telling the truth. He absorbed the cold and said, "Come on, Biggie, what kind of idiot would I have to be to lie to you?"

Biggie Mann smiled. "A very large one," he said.

"If I had it to do over again, I'd take a phone selfie with the package on the porch to prove I left it there. If you want me to drop another bomb I'll do it, no additional charge. This time I will take a picture."

Biggie lobbed another grape into his mouth, chewed for a moment, and then said, "Fine. Do it." Then he swiveled his chair in order to look out the window at West L.A. far below.

Feeling things had gone even better than he expected, Lou Beratti silently got up and went to the elevator, punching the only button. When it arrived, he stepped in.

By the time he realized the floor of the elevator car was now an open trap, he'd already plummeted six stories. The muffled thud came even before the elevator doors closed again.

"They'll be on the lookout for something now, idiot," Biggie Mann said to no one. He had been forced into a corner with only one option left. Picking up his desk phone, the big man punched in a number, and said, "Get the plane ready to fly out eight this evening. Oh, and cleanup on aisle five." Then he hung up.

Pulling out a prepaid phone, he thumbed in another number and waited. "Got a job for you," he said, going on to explain in detail what he wanted. When he was finished, he cut off the call, put the phone on the floor and stomped it to bits, which he scooped up and threw away.

Let the Sowl woman testify against him; he'll be gone and she'll be dead in a matter of days.

If you can't actually kill a witness prior to her testimony, Biggie Mann rationalized, you can at least send a message to others.

Having watched television her entire life, Marie Finnerman knew that in any murder case the spouse immediately becomes the prime suspect, but she seemed to be cleared fairly quickly. She had been so distraught and uncomprehending that even the most expert interrogators were convinced. What's more, there was no financial incentive for the killing. The Finnerman family had been surviving largely on Bruce's unemployment insurance since his layoff five months ago and there was no big payday life insurance policy. Neither was there any evidence of a girlfriend or a second family, non-financial reasons for Marie to want him dead. Even if she had for some as yet undiscovered reason, a package bomb was probably the least likely way for her to do it, if for no other reason because it might inadvertently hurt the kids.

So weary had she grown of talking to various members of the police department that Marie thought about ignoring the doorbell when it rang on Saturday morning and pretending she was not home. Then a call came in on her cell from a Detective Jen Hahn, who informed her she was standing outside. Reluctantly, Marie opened the door to see a young, smiling, non-uniformed woman flashing a badge. "I don't know that there's anything more I can tell you people," she said.

"Well, I have a specific request," Detective Hahn replied. "Your husband had a personal computer, right?"

"Yes, a laptop. Why?"

"Can you access it?"

"I'd have to find it first. I haven't really thought about it since …"

"Please try, if you would."

"Is it important?"

"It might be crucial."

After letting the policewoman in, Marie began searching the house for the computer, only to come up empty. "I don't understand," she said. "I used to see him use it all the time. Now it's gone."

"Could it possibly be in the garage?" Detective Hahn asked.

"I don't know why, but I'll look."

For obvious reasons Marie did not like going into the garage anymore, and even kept the family car parked outside in the driveway. But only a cursory glance at the still damaged space revealed Bruce's laptop case to be leaning up against a large plastic tool shed he'd bought several months ago. Carrying it inside, she set it down on the living room coffee table and plugged in the power cord, assuming the battery had run out. She thought she remembered Bruce's login ID and password, but it still took a half-dozen variable tries before getting in. "Okay, what do you need to see?" Marie asked Detective Hahn.

"Emails," the policewoman replied. "We need to check if there are any threatening ones."

"If there were, he probably would have deleted them."

"Right, but deleting an active email only sends it to another file."

Fortunately Bruce had his email ID and password automatically saved, so Marie had no trouble getting to his inbox. "Looks like spam for the most part," she said. "House refi, computer security system upsell, stuff like ... wait, what's this?"

Detective Hahn moved behind the sofa so as to peer over her shoulder.

Still waiting was in the subject line of a message from someone named Bram Trindle. Opening it up, she read:

Dear Mr. Finnerman:

It has been three weeks now since I made the winning bid on the mini pedal exerciser and paid the $210 into your account and to date I have not received the item, which you listed as (and which I paid for) 2-to-5 day delivery. If I have not received the item by Monday, I plan to file a complaint with eBay, which will undoubtedly lower your satisfaction rating. I am sorry to be so insistent, but my patience is running thin.

"I don't understand this at all," Marie said. "I never knew Bruce to use eBay, and even if he had, we don't own a portable exerciser."

"Do you have a PayPal site?" the detective asked.

"Not that I know of."

"Go on and see."

Connecting to the PayPal site, Marie hit the login button and found that Bruce's information was once again saved. Clicking the login button, she waited only a second until Bruce's account information came up.

Marie Finnerman gasped as she read: *Money is waiting for you—$46,391.*

A vengeance job carried a higher price tag than a simple hit because of the inherent risk. At least he had a little time: the trial of Biggie Mann on income tax evasion, including the testimony of CPA Elena Sowl, was recessed once it was discovered that Biggie had skipped town. But chances were excellent that the authorities were placing the woman under constant protection, just in case.

Pedo (short for *torpedo*) sat in his stolen car down the street from Elena Sowl's small Pacoima house, attentively watching through tiny binoculars. There were no overt signs of a police presence, but they had to be there somewhere. Understanding that they were very likely looking back from the cover of the house Pedo pulled away from the curb after only a couple minutes and drove off. He'd come back tomorrow with a new jacked vehicle so his wheels wouldn't be recognized.

That could not be said for the black sedan with muni plates and a visible spotlight that Pedo passed on the next block, which was quite possibly the most obvious unmarked police car he'd ever seen. Pulling into a driveway to turn around, he followed the car until it pulled up to the curb in front of the target house. One man in a business suit got out and went to the house while another one stayed inside the car.

Man, they weren't even trying to hide.

Maybe that was the answer!

The old hide-in-plain-sight trick, he thought, realizing how simple it would be. If Biggie Mann knew how simple this would be, he'd probably stiff him on the payoff.

But then Biggie wasn't around to contribute input. He was hiding out somewhere in Canada, waiting for all this to be over.

At least he's getting some good whisky, Pedo thought as he drove past the soon-to-be dead woman's house.

Marie stared at the computer screen uncomprehendingly.

Computers;

Exercise equipment;

Expensive clothing;

Jewelry;

A television;

Toys;

Books and DVDs;

Vitamin supplements;

Baby goods;

Marie couldn't believe the sheer volume of things Bruce had sold online over the last seven months. He was always a packrat, saving receipts, bills, even things like junk fliers in the mail. It sometimes drove Marie crazy. In this instance he had records of each item, the date he put it up for sale, the starting price, the winning bid, the date payment was received, and the shipping cost—everything except information about the buyers. Maybe that was kept in a separate file somewhere.

What would be even more illuminating, though, was information regarding where Bruce got all the stuff he'd sold to the tune of $40-thousand in the first place.

That was when the truth hit Marie like a pinecone from a tree. She suddenly understood why Bruce had spent so much time by himself working on his laptop, why he had gone out and bought that portable storage shed and put it in the garage, and why he spent so many afternoons out "running errands." Why had she not paid more attention to what he was doing earlier?

Had she, he might still be alive.

Steeling herself to go out to the garage, she wrenched open the door of his plastic storage unit and found inside a large box that had survived the explosion with only minimal damage. A photo was printed onto it, that of a man using some kind of pedal exercise device.

"Dammit, Bruce," she uttered before going back into the house to phone the police. Asking for Detective Hahn, she was forced to wait a minute before the woman's voice came on. "I think I know what my husband was doing," Marie said, fighting back tears. "I think when he wasn't able to find another job he became a porch pirate, stealing packages wherever he could find them and then selling them online."

"I was working toward the same conclusion," Hahn replied. "In fact, I've been going through a stack of reports regarding stolen goods. I've made a list of them."

Comparing the items listed off by the detective to the items Marie found on Bruce's list, they found enough matches to make their suspicions a certainty. "What do we do now?" Marie asked.

"You can check to see if any more disgruntled customers try to contact your husband through email, while I contact everyone who filed a report and give them the bad news," Detective Hahn said. "Then I'll go back to the bomb squad and see if they've turned up any kind of evidence to tell us where your husband might have found his last package."

"Does that matter at this point?"

"Well, yes, because whoever it is was the real target of the bomb. I'd like to know why."

"That won't bring Bruce back."

"Agreed, but it might save someone else and lead us to the person who sent the bomb in the first place. You do want to see your husband's killer apprehended, don't you?"

"Of course. But finding that particular porch sounds like kind of a long shot."

There was a long pause at the other end of the phone connection before Marie heard, "I'd use the word unlikely, Mrs. Finnerman, but I have to try."

"Hey, Jen, you need to see this," Detective Carl Amato said, poking his head into her cubicle. Hahn took a break from her crippling paperwork and followed him into a room that had a video set up. "This is a video file that was emailed to us from a woman in Pacoima. She's been noticing a lot of activity at the house across the street, and went back to look at her own porch camera footage, which shows the front of her neighbor's place. Watch."

The detectives looked at the monitor and saw a white van pull up to the curb across the street, the driver get out, and a box being delivered on the porch. Then the driver, whose face was obscured by shades and a hat, practically ran back to the van and took off.

"Now this is several hours later," Amato said, pointing out the cut in the footage. Another van drove by slowly, then stopped and backed up, parking at the curb. The driver leapt out, leaving the door open, looked around, ran up to the house, grabbed the package, and ran back to the van and tossed it in.

"Looks like we've found our porch pirate," Hahn said. "Is there any way we can clarify this image so we can see who it is?"

"We can do even better than that," Amato said. "The van pulled out, then made a U in the street and pulled into the driveway of the neighbor with the security camera, coming close enough to it to get a good read on the license plate."

"Hot diggety damn," Hahn said, jotting down the number. It took exactly 49 seconds on the DMV database to reveal the van belonged to Bruce Finnerman. A rush of relief flowed through her. "Now the question is why the person in that house had a bomb delivered to them in the first place?"

"Asked and answered," Amato replied with a grin, handing her a sheet of paper. "You're gonna love this."

Taking out the mail carrier, peeling off his uniform, and stealing his truck were so easy Pedo wondered why he never thought of it before. It took a few minutes to get used to the right-hand drive of the vehicle, but he managed. Since time was of the essence, he drove straight to the street on which Elena Sowl lived and parked at the corner. Grabbing a handful of mail from the tray next to him, Pedo made a show of stopping at each house and dropping some of it off. He had no idea whose mail it was and he really didn't care. It was all for show for whomever was watching.

When he got to the Sowl place he walked up to the door and knocked, then reached into his pocket with a gloved hand and withdrew his gun, which was already muffled, hiding it behind the fistful of mail. While it was SOP to empty the entire clip into a target, Pedo knew he had only one shot at the target. That's the way the scenario he'd devised played out.

He'd put one bullet through her heart and then shove the gun back into the pocket of his ridiculous gray postal shorts, after which he'd scream when she fell and wait for the cops inside to appear. Then he'd claim that he turned and saw a man across the street with a rifle running away. Then he'd tear back down to the mail truck and speed off, park it somewhere, change back into his own clothes, and walk away. By the time they realized there was no phantom rifleman, he'd be long gone.

It was perfect in its simplicity.

"Who is it?" a woman's voice called through the door.

"Mailman, special delivery," Pedo responded.

The door creaked open and half of a woman's face appeared. "I'm not expecting a special delivery."

"Sorry, ma'am, but it has to be signed for."

"Hold on."

The door closed again and Pedo waited tensely. Her closing the door on him had not been part of his scenario. He was considering aborting the mission and trying again later when the door opened fully up.

"Sorry, I had to get a pen," she said.

"Not a problem," Pedo replied, revealing the gun and firing one shot straight at her heart. The woman collapsed like a felled tree.

Pocketing the gun, Pedo turned around and shouted, "My God, he shot her! That man!"

But no police officers came rushing from the house.

He shouted again to no avail. Had he been wrong about police protection? Could it be that given Biggie Mann's flight, the court assumed she'd be safe on her own after all?

Either way it was not his problem; the job had been fulfilled. He started toward the mail van only to encounter a half-dozen plainclothes officers leaping out of various unmarked cars lining the street, each one leveling a gun at him.

"On the ground, now!" one in front demanded, and with so many gun barrels trained on him, Pedo had no choice but to comply. As his wrists were being cuffed behind him, he saw the woman he had moments before shot through the heart walk into his line of vision.

"Damn, I wish someone had told me how much it would hurt even through a Kevlar vest," said Detective Jen Hahn, massaging her breast.

Jen Hahn was relieved to learn that her ribs were only bruised, not broken.

Pedo … whose real name was Jason Costello … cut a deal and turned state's evidence in return for a reduced charge. For Costello, though, the bitterest pill was hearing the laughter from the D.A.'s people when they told him that his "brilliantly simple" plan to get near Elena Sowl contained a fatal flaw: under advice from the authorities, she had shut off her mail delivery until further notice. Pretending to deliver mail to her was how the hitman gave himself away.

It only took three weeks for Biggie Mann to be tracked down in Toronto and apprehended. Once he was back in California, Elena Sowl gave her testimony in regards to the original charges. For his subsequent trial on murder and attempted murder charges, Mann (whose real name was Bernard Levon) would have Costello and Detective Jen Hahn on the witness list.

None of this, however, spared Marie Finnerman and her children from their loss, their financial problems, or the threat of legal action from her husband's illicit activities. She was in danger of losing the house until a package, slightly larger than a shoebox, arrived one day on the porch. Upon finding it, she immediately called Detective Hahn who told her to leave the house at once, and arrived in short order with the bomb squad. Once examination proved the package was harmless, Hahn carried it inside the house and opened it. Marie Finnerman yelped like she'd been tased when she saw the stacks of hundred dollar bills stuffed inside.

"There's a note tucked in the side," Jen Hahn said, pulling out a small sheet of yellow lined paper.

Dear Mrs. Finnerman, it read;

You don't know me, but I've been following the story of my rotten ex Bernie, who you know better as 'Biggie Mann.' I'm glad they finally got the bastard! I know what it's like to be lied to by a husband. Bernie didn't think I knew where he hid his "petty cash," but I did. He kept it in that house in Ontario that he ran to every time he got in trouble. Big man, huh? Tries to kill a woman and then runs like a rabbit when he fails. Anyway, he won't need money where he's going, but it sounds like you do. So please take this as a gift from me, and don't worry. It's all legal. Not marked or anything.

Take care of your little ones.

The letter was signed *Sophia Levon.*
"I can't keep this," Marie said. "Oh, God, I want to, but I can't, right?"
"I don't know why not," Hahn replied.

"How can you say that? What if it's stolen loot?"

"The woman said it wasn't. She's the only one with first-hand knowledge of it."

"I don't know ..."

"It's not like you stole this package off of someone's porch."

"You're not going to tell anyone about this, are you?" Marie asked.

The detective rose to leave. "Look, Mrs. Finnerman, I work homicide. If you have evidence that Ben Franklin was murdered a thousand times and turned into little green slips of paper, maybe I'll get involved. Otherwise, why not take some of that and fix your garage door?"

TWO SHARKS WALK INTO A BAR

David Krugler

Carol's Pub had the sorriest, most raggedy-assed pool table Meredith had ever seen. The felt was scuffed, nicked, and stained; the cushions, battered and uneven. A folded piece of cardboard—torn from the lid of a beer bottle case—leveled one leg on the warped linoleum flooring. The pocket points were misaligned and two had hairline cracks. Cigarette burns marred the edging, dark welts curling like sneers from the composite plastic.

The location befit the table's condition. Way back of the tavern, wedged into a nook haphazardly created by a windowless brick wall, walk-in cooler, and broom-and-mop rack. A narrow plywood mantel for bottles and ashtrays jutted from the brick wall. A faded Bicentennial banner sagged from two nails. Someone had penned a mustache on George Washington, a beard on Thomas Jefferson, and goggles on Benjamin Franklin. Four stools with ripped cushions, a Pabst light with fringed shade, and two long-haired punks in Levis, T-shirts, and neck chains completed the décor.

Punk One was taking a shot. A hard left cut on the seven ball into a side pocket. Meredith didn't watch the balls. She took in his stance, grip, elbow angle, and bridge, keeping her eyes on the cue's glide as he shot. Smooth, not too hard, but with a wobble. Unconsciously, he slipped his bridge as he finished, probably because he was thinking too hard about keeping his right elbow aligned with the cue. He still dropped the seven ball, left himself good for a corner pocket kiss on the one ball.

"Is the girls' room back here?" Meredith asked before he could shoot. She put the slightest lilt into her voice, just a hint of Laverne and Shirley, while looking around quizzically.

The shooter looked up from the table. Punk Two perched on a stool with his boots hooked on its rail, cue in hand. They scoped her out, squinting through the bangs drifting over their eyebrows. Punk Two took a theatrical drag on his king-size.

"Nah, babe, s'round the bar, back that'a way," he drawled, gesturing vaguely.

The Southern accent gave him away as a recent arrival in Chicago. Carol's, a honky-tonk joint, was in Uptown, a beatdown neighborhood recently taking in lots of poor whites from Appalachia.

"Thanks!" She twirled around and returned to the bar where Darren was waiting. For this job, Meredith wore shorts, a fitted tee, and flats. July, and the city was as humid as a jungle. Just about every other woman in the bar wore a similar outfit. Darren wanted her to wear stiletto heels with straps. *Meri, you flex your right foot when you're shooting, let him see that shoe dangle just so, for sure he won't be thinking about his next shot!* Took her five minutes to explain why stiletto heels with straps didn't go with shorts and a tee. Maybe they would find a mark with a foot fetish. Or maybe the mark would wonder why the hell she was sporting those shoes and tumble to the ploy.

Meredith slid onto the stool Darren had been guarding for her.

"Table?" he asked.

"About fell off a dump truck."

"Rough, huh."

"Worse than Canton."

"Jeez. Natives?"

"Two hillbillies."

He smirked. "Your people. Maybe they're your second cousins."

"Wouldn't that be something?" Meredith decided to say. She had worked hard to lose her accent, but Darren still teased her about being from Kentucky.

"Sandbag 'em?" he asked.

"Too obvious."

"Rope-a-Dope?"

"Thought about it, but no."

"Explain."

"Pro: They're young and think they're hot shit. One I saw shoot, s'got a wobble. We could work that. Con: They know better than to bang those beat-up rails."

"Try a Bicker?"

"They'll just bail."

"For Chrissake, then what?"

That edge to his voice, already—they weren't ten minutes in yet. Darren's nerves were fraying a lot lately.

"I'm thinking we could—"

"What can I getcha, hon?" the barmaid interjected. Like the two pool players, she had a Southern accent.

"Rum and coke, lotsa ice," Meredith answered.

"Sure thing."

Turning back to Darren, Meredith said, "Dazzle, we should go with that."

"For real?"

"Yep."

He didn't respond. Took a long drink of his Miller High Life, drew on his Kent, blew smoke. Then:

"I need to see for myself."

"No."

"No?" The edge had sharpened.

Meredith put on a smile, squeezed his bicep. "I already asked if the bathrooms were back there. You take a look now and then we ask to play, they'll know we've been checking them out. You gotta trust me on this, Dare-bear."

"Dare-bear, ain't that sweet," the barmaid said with a big grin, setting down Meredith's drink. She looked to be on the right side of forty, hair piled high and tied with a checked handkerchief, sleeves rolled on plump arms.

Meredith flinched, worried Darren would lose his temper because his pet-name had been overheard, but he smiled and held out his palms. "Yep, I'm just a big ole sack of sugar, Ma'am," he said.

"You're a big ole sumpin-sumpin, that's for sure," the barmaid said, admiring Darren's broad shoulders and powerful chest. No doubt about it, Darren was handsome, strong jaw and planed cheeks, just enough rough touches—bump on the bridge of his nose, crooked eyebrows—to keep him from being a pretty boy.

The barmaid took a dollar from their bills on the bar and headed to the cash register.

"So, no Sandbag, no Rope-a-Dope, no Bicker," Darren said. "Dazzle. I don't know ..."

The Sandbag was a tried-and-true hustle. Grab a warped house cue, let the mark see that. Make a shot now and then, near-miss others, selling it (a groan, a curse, a look of self-disgust) so the mark doesn't notice he's getting left with not-so-easy shots. Throw the first two games, win the third with a "lucky" shot. Scratch on the eight ball to finish the fourth, beg for a rematch. No scratch this time.

Rope-a-Dope was Darren's creation, named after Ali and Foreman's famous bout. Darren came out shooting hard, muscling the cue and deliberately slamming the pocket points off-center so the balls careened right out. Without realizing it, the marks also started hitting hard, some kind of macho reflex, as if they couldn't let big ole Darren look stronger than them. On the fifth game, Darren "suddenly" found his aim, nailing the balls dead center.

In Bicker, she and Darren played doubles and sniped at one another about misses, giving each other dirty looks as the insults got more barbed before they "made up" and took game five. Acting-wise, the Bicker was easy—Darren's folks had split when he was ten, Meredith's when she was twelve.

Dazzle was Meredith's baby. Took a certain type of mark. Young, loaded, arrogant. A guy who hated to lose. Especially to a woman. Meredith would prime the mark by whispering to Darren, who would shake his head.

"What?" the mark would ask.

"She wants to play you solo."

"So?"

Then Darren would tell him how much money Meredith wanted to bet. That put the mark on the spot but good. Back down from playing a girl, look chicken? Darren had to be smart, name a figure at the outer limit of what he guessed the mark was carrying. Every time they had run Dazzle, he'd always hooked the mark, who put up all his cash. And Meredith had won every time. No holding back, as in Sandbag or Bicker—she went straight for the kill, working to run the table from her first shot. Darren had dubbed it Dazzle for Meredith's ability to plot out her seven shots from the get-go, the way she'd skip the obvious makes to do a reverse bank or a tricky combo, all to set herself up for the run. Despite his admiration, Darren always resisted going with Dazzle. Not only did it sideline him, he didn't like the idea of all their cash riding on Meredith's cue.

"How you gonna run Dazzle on two marks?" he now said truculently. "What if you can't cut the weaker one from his partner?"

Don't push it, Meredith told herself. "Okay, no Dazzle," she said. "Maybe we could Bicker them, if we ease into it, keep it light."

He nodded briskly, stubbed his cigarette. "Let's do that."

She sipped her drink, didn't respond, keeping her gaze on the mirrored backbar. Darren caught her look in the reflection.

"What?"

"Nothing."

He sighed impatiently. "What aren't you saying, Meri?"

"It's just ... well, okay, I keep thinking about the transmission."

"Dammit, you know better'n that." Darren grabbed his cigarettes, tapped out another Kent, snapped open his Zippo.

"I know, I know, I shouldn't have brought it up. Forget I said anything."

An ironclad rule: never, ever hustle because you're desperate. Even the best player could psych himself out that way. *Need fifty bucks to make the rent ... fridge is bare-ass empty ...* Or, as Meredith and Darren had found out that morning, they needed 282 dollars to replace the transmission on Darren's 1967 Nova. Meredith had noticed the clanking when they left Canton, every time she shifted. You hear that? she had asked Darren. Hear what? He was cranky, trying to crib a nap while she drove. That clanking, she'd said. I don't hear shit, he'd answered. She'd persisted, slowed the car, told him to downshift into fourth while she kept the clutch in. He'd done it, clumsily, because he was using his left hand. Gear box feels tight, doesn't it? she'd asked. I guess so, he'd said. Darren liked fast cars, but he didn't know anything about them. Meredith's dad, a mechanic, had taken her to his shop when he had visitation; she knew engines. She'd gotten the repair quote from the first shop they saw once they hit Chicago. The car was drivable, short-term, but they couldn't leave town without the repair. Pushing Dazzle just to get that 282 dollars—that was bad luck, as she'd just admitted to Darren. He was in no mood for an apology though.

"Can I count on you or what? You gonna play your part?" About to lose his temper.

"Yeah, you can count on me," she shot back. "How 'bout you? Maybe you oughta lay off that beer, your hand looks a little shaky."

In an instant, that look. Eyes flashing, jaw clenching, shoulder and bicep muscles going taut. As he released a gritted hiss, Meredith flashed a smile.

"See, babe? Just practicing the Bicker."

Darren relaxed, allowed himself a grin. "Oh, that was a good one, Meri, you really had me there for a second."

"It's one of our best acts, isn't it? The Bicker."

"Never let us down yet."

"I never failed on Dazzle yet, either."

"Meri, c'mon ..."

She put her hand on his thigh, leaned to whisper. "We'll do whatever you want, Dare-Bear. All I'm saying is, see what you think after you get a look at these two. I think they're here warming up on this rat-trap of a table so they can hustle someplace else. Which means they're carrying a lotta bread."

"All right, I'll think about it. Follow my lead."

"Always, always."

The punk Meredith had seen shooting said his name was Lester. His boots put him a tick over six feet. Lean torso, ropy muscles, faint freckling on his cheeks. His hands were chafed, grime under his nails. His buddy Virgil was a few inches shorter, with a squat build, short arms, and thick wrists. He sported a bristly mustache under a pug nose. Meredith hoped Darren saw what she saw: both men had telltale wads of cash in the front pockets of their jeans. Maybe, just maybe, he'd go for the Dazzle if the Bicker worked out.

"Yeah, sure," Lester answered Darren's suggestion they play doubles. He didn't say anything about money and neither did Darren.

"Find the little girls' room, little lady?" Virgil asked, laughing at his joke.

"Oh, sure, thanks for the directions!" Meredith smiled, playing along.

Darren racked for eight ball. She reached for a cue.

"Let me do that," Darren commanded. "You don't know anything about pool sticks." The opening ruse: boss her around. He held a cue out and peered down its shaft, looking for a warp. Lester and Virgil had brought custom cues, the cases stacked on the wall shelf. They exchanged looks as Darren proclaimed, "This'll do."

Virgil broke hard, careened the three ball straight into the right corner pocket at the foot of the table. The spread left him an easy shot on the six ball in the left corner, but then he missed cutting the one into the left side pocket. "Awwh, hell," he groaned. "I shoulda made that."

Meredith noticed Virgil left the cue ball tight against the rail, without a clear shot for them. A classic Sandbag—the hillbillies were trying to hustle them. But the Bicker played well against a Sandbag. Nothing like a couple arguing to create a distraction.

"So we're the stripey balls, right, hon?" Meredith asked as Darren stood to take his turn.

"Obviously," he answered sarcastically. He made a show of studying the leave: squatting down to scrutinize the rail, staring at various stripes. He came down hard on the cue ball from an awkward angle. The tip glanced off and struck the felt—a scratch.

"Oops," Meredith giggled.

He glared. "You think you coulda done better?"

So much for easing into it, keeping the squabble light.

"We'll see, won't we?"

Lester shot next. Sunk the one ball his partner had missed, then tried a reverse bank on the four that came up short, intentionally. He left Meredith two clean shots, one easier than the other. Which one she took would tell him and Virgil a lot. If she took the hard shot, a cut on the twelve, she'd set herself up for a good run, at least three more balls, and they'd know she could shoot. The sure shot, on the fourteen, would leave her behind the eight ball. "Recon," she and Darren called this ploy, furtively setting up your opponent so you could appraise them. Time to mess with their heads, she thought.

She studied the lay, then looked expectantly at Darren. "I'm thinking I should try for this purple one"—she pointed at the twelve—"cuz then I can—"

"No, no, no!" Darren jumped up from his stool, immediately sensing what she was up to. "You can't make that shot. Take the fourteen." He grabbed the cue from her hands and pantomimed the shot for her.

"Are you sure?"

"Yes—do it already!"

Meredith shot, sank the fourteen. Predictably, the cue ball settled an inch behind the eight. Now the hustle was primed. Virgil and Lester could see she knew how to read the table but that her boyfriend was too dense to give her a chance. Hopefully, that would embolden them to casually propose playing for money, especially once she and Darren really started to bicker.

And bicker they did, for the rest of that game and straight through the next, Darren laying it on strong, telling her she shot like a girl and coming over to arrange her stance and shot, moving her arms around as if she was a rag doll. For her part, Meredith started pushing back, changing her compliance to petulance, then irritation. "Well, you're not making your shots either" ... "I didn't have anything to shoot at!" They lost the first game, and the second. Darren pounded the cue on the floor. "Well, this is a waste of time. C'mon, let's go," he snapped at Meredith.

Lester piped up. "No, man, this is fun. Maybe we oughta make the next game a little interesting, whattya say?"

"You mean like for money?" Darren laughed derisively, jerked his head toward Meredith. "You think I'm gonna play for money with her as my partner?" He ostentatiously took out his wallet, extended it. "Why don't you just help yourself and get it over with?"

Darren's acting was good. Too good, Meredith thought. But she stayed in character, lowering her head at his abuse.

"Well, we could handicap," Lester said.

"How's that?"

"After the break, we'll take two of your balls off the table straightaway."

Darren pretended to think about the offer. "Three. You saw how lousy she is."

Lester looked at Virgil, who nodded and said, "Fifty bucks a game."

"Sure."

"Rack 'em," Lester told Darren.

They threw that game, but Darren eased up toward the end, stopped dictating her shots, stopped belittling her. When she sunk a ball, he offered grudging praise. Darren put another fifty up; they lost it.

"Double-or-nothing?" Lester asked casually.

"You mean a hundred?"

Lester ticked his chin.

"We're still handicapping, right?"

"Yep."

"Well, man, I—oh hell, why not?" Darren bent to retrieve the rack.

Showtime for Meredith. They needed to win, but if Darren upped his game, the hillbillies would catch on and refuse a rematch. If Lester and Virgil quit after losing this game, she and Darren only broke even. Another double-or-nothing—200 dollars—almost fetched them what they needed for the car. Don't think that, she rebuked herself. She needed to stay deep in the hustle, concentrate on looking like an amateur on a lucky streak ...

"I made it, I made it!" She squealed with delight as she just—*just*—dropped the eight ball in the side pocket on her third turn, after clearing their last ball off the table. Darren had played masterfully, sinking only one or two each turn, always leaving Virgil with a tough shot. Meredith brought the cue ball perilously close to the pocket, counting on the rough felt to stop it from following the eight ball in.

"You almost scratched," Darren glowered.

Meredith's face fell. Was he still in character, pushing the hillbillies to believe that she would start missing after being rebuked, or did he mean it? Too often, the Bicker started to feel real.

"Good game," Virgil said flatly.

"Guess that makes us even," Lester said, handing over a hundred dollars. As Darren slipped the bills into his front pocket, Lester asked, "Want to go again? "

"How much?"

"Thought we agreed on double-or-nothing the last round."

"So two hundred?"

"That's double a hundred, ain't it?"

Darren ignored the crack. "All right—rack 'em."

"No handicap this time," Virgil piped up from his stool.

"You're the ones suggested it," Darren protested.

"Sure. But the little lady's on a roll now. Cain't expect us to play for two-hundred bucks with y'all three balls ahead."

Darren appeared to think, then leveled his gaze at Meredith. "You better play good."

"I will," she shot back.

And did she ever, Darren too. They were all-in now. Meredith lived for this moment, when she could stop missing, could shrug off the ditz act; and she could shoot to kill. The Bicker was off—she and Darren were a team again. They had to put these hillbillies down, just like they'd put the two ironworkers down in Canton on the eleventh game of nine ball, clearing 160 dollars; just like they'd taken the sixth game in Cincinnati the week before in a fierce round of Rope-a-Dope. When all the money was on the line, they both came alive, prowling the table, chalk squeaking as they readied their cues, single-minded and relentless, pouncing on every ball like panthers on prey. Darren was one of the finest short game players she'd ever seen, since she took to hanging out in her Uncle Filbert's pool hall after her folks split up. Sure-footed, a power-hitter with admirable control.

For her part, Meredith had a glide as straight as a rifle shot. She could take a ball clear across the green, drop it without fail, never needing a friendly roll off the pocket point. And her leaves! As Darren said, the night they met and she took him for 300 bucks, she could read the table like a book. More like a board, she liked to think, chess being the other game her Uncle Filbert had taught her. Always thinking several shots ahead, surveying the spread, seeing her balls as pieces to move around the table, which is why she could pull off the Dazzle. She was good on her own, but a solo hustle as a woman was difficult and dangerous. Constantly being hit on and pawed, never knowing when a mark might get violent. She had already had two close scrapes when she hooked up with Darren. For a while, they'd been good together, and not just on the pool table. Then Darren started losing his temper over the littlest things. His beer wasn't cold enough, she'd left a towel on the hotel bathroom floor. Whatever was eating him, he wouldn't say, but he was getting moodier and more unpredictable. As the bruise on her right forearm kept reminding her.

"Awwh, Goddammit all," Virgil groaned as Darren dropped the eight ball into a corner pocket. He handed over 200 dollars and sullenly watched Darren pocket the cash.

"I'm done," Lester said, unscrewing his custom cue.

"You cain't quit on me now, partner," Virgil protested.

"You wanna play, keep playin', I ain't gonna stop you."

The perfect set-up! Meredith jumped up from her stool, ran over to Darren, and whispered into his ear. "Let's go big, baby, let's do the Dazzle."

He scowled and shook his head. "No, I don't think so."

Was he playing along or really saying no? Meredith couldn't tell.

"What?" Virgil asked.

"She wants, well, she wants to play more doubles."

So he *was* nixing the Dazzle. Couldn't he see how easily she could beat Virgil?

Virgil said, "Well man, I cain't play doubles without a partner," giving Lester a dismissive nod. "But how about you and me play one-on-one, big man? Maybe a little nine ball?"

It was like he wanted to hand his cash over to them! All Darren had to say was, 'Sure, but why don't you play her instead?' Meredith could stroke a nine-ball rack like a yo-yo: up, down, and all the way around.

But Darren didn't say that. What he said was, "If I'm gonna play you solo, it's gotta be worth my while." His gaze flickered over the thick pad of bills still evident in Virgil's front pocket.

Meredith didn't let her face show what she was thinking. Nine ball was not Darren's best game.

Virgil smiled. "You wanna bet big, you mean."

Darren nodded.

Virgil didn't say anything for a moment. The bar had become louder—a country band was playing up front. Cigarette smoke hung heavy in the air, the Pabst light over the pool table made jerky rotations, hueing the scuffed felt in a pale red circle. Taking a long drag on his cigarette, Virgil said, "Awright man, you wanna up the stakes, you got it. Why don't we play for something you cain't afford to lose?"

"Yeah? What's that?"

Another drag, exhale. When the smoke cleared from his face, Virgil pointed at Meredith:

"Her."

Meredith let out a shocked yelp.

Darren laughed. "Funny."

"I ain't joshin' ya."

"That is not cool, you understand?" Darren squared his shoulders and took a step toward Virgil.

Who didn't back down. "Don't you wanna know what I'm gonna put up?"

Darren shook his head but Virgil spoke anyway.

"My ride, that's what I'll put up." He reached into his pocket and took out a key ring, jangled it. "Oughta come take a look, man, it's a sweet machine."

Darren looked over at Meredith, who had lowered her head, hands clenched in her lap. She could break character, she knew. Just stand up and say, "No way, we're done." Or should she stay quiet, see how Darren played it? He might convince Virgil to stick with cash—double-or-nothing would put 400 dollars on the table. So long as he didn't think about how the Nova needed a new transmission, and he didn't agree to see the car.

"I'm not saying yes, understand? But I'll look at your car."

Meredith jumped up, ran over and grabbed his forearm. "Baby, no, you can't—"

He shrugged her off. "We're just taking a look, okay, nobody's bet nothing."

"I don't care, you can't do this!"

But Darren was already following Virgil and Lester out the bar's side door. Meredith hurried after them. The street was narrow and lined with parked cars. The canopies of ash and elm trees arched over the pavement. Brick apartment buildings and cut stone single-family homes loomed behind high iron fences. *No Trespassing* signs abounded, as did alarm company shields with silhouetted pistols or German shepherds. Virgil led them down the block and greeted a teen with unruly curls falling past his shoulders. He was perched on a milk crate upturned on the government strip.

"Any trouble, Duane?"

"Naw."

"My sister's kid," Virgil explained. "Cain't leave a car like mine unattended 'round these parts."

Darren wasn't listening. He was all-eyes on a 1975 Pontiac Firebird, cherry red with a black stenciled phoenix spreading its wings just below the hood header. Rally II rims, whitewall Goodrich radials, black leather bucket seats, six-speed transmission, power windows. The setting sun, slanting through the shade trees, brightened the waxed finish. Darren ran his finger along the edge of the driver side door, peering into the interior.

"You got papers?" he asked.

Meredith's stomach heaved. He was going to take the bet! She rushed over. "Dare-Bear, we should—"

"Right here." Virgil tugged a worn, folded sheet from his wallet. Darren studied the title and handed it back.

"Darren!"

"Gimme a moment, yeah?" he said to Virgil, who nodded.

Darren guided Meredith behind the nearest tree.

"We should do it," he whispered. "I won't lose, I promise." Stroking her hand, like a nervous beau about to propose.

"Are you outta your mind? You can't treat me like a hunk of meat!"

"I won't lose, baby."

"What if you do?"

He squeezed her hand. "Then we'll cut and run."

She jerked free. "You don't think they'll be ready for that? Lester'll be on me like white on rice."

"I won't lose, baby," he said again.

"No. I don't wanna do it."

He gently lifted her chin with his fingers, looked into her eyes. "Trust me. I got this. One game'a nine-ball and that car's ours."

She met his gaze. They weren't supposed to think about the prizes before they played, were they?

"Promise you won't leave me, no matter what."

"I promise. But I'm not going to lose. Believe you me, I got this hillbilly's number."

Darren's table, his break. He barely kissed the one bill, nudging the rack, leaving no leaves. But Virgil understood that opener, kissed the one ball right back. Darren brought it out and dropped it with a masterful massé. He was just able to nick the two ball, but the hillbilly wedged the two ball right back in the rack and back-spun the cue ball into the kitchen. Darren couldn't hit the two ball, so Virgil had ball-in-hand—he could put the cue ball wherever he wanted. He lined himself up for another kiss of the two and again back-spun the cue ball into the kitchen.

Meredith saw what was happening—Virgil was running his own Rope-a-Dope, in reverse! Toying with Darren, pushing him toward a hard shot just to break up the rack. If he did that, the way Virgil had composed the lay, the seven ball would push the nine toward the corner pocket and leave the two on a straight line toward the nine. In this game, you didn't have to sink the balls in numerical order to win, not if you slopped, bumped, or banged the nine ball in any way you could.

Meredith licked dry lips. "Hey, baby, before—"

Crack! Darren muscled his shot, breaking up the clustered balls. They veered this way and that, in seemingly random directions, but just as she feared, the two ball left a clear shot on the nine.

Darren stared at the table, too stunned even to swear. He wiped his brow.

"Well, would you look at that?" Virgil said, chalking his cue. But he wasn't looking at the table—he was staring at Meredith. Lester had sidled into the passageway to the bar, blocking the only exit.

"Listen, man, you gotta gimme another chance, another game—"

"Hold your horses now, I gotta make the shot," Virgil said. He bent over the table, shot carefully and slowly. The nine ball dropped with a thud.

"No, no, no," Meredith whimpered.

"Another game, we have to play again," Darren insisted. "I let you play after you lost."

"How we gonna go double-or-nothing now? I ain't got but one car, and less your pretty little lady's got a twin, you only got one'a her."

Meredith ran to Darren and jumped on him, wrapping her arms and legs around him. "Get me outta here, you promised!" she hissed into his ear.

"Okay, okay, I won't let them take you," he whispered. He nudged her off, getting her feet on the floor. Her hands dropped to his waist, letting go slowly. Virgil and Lester stood side-by-side in the doorway, arms crossed.

"Now look," Darren began nervously. "This bet, you know we were just joking around, right? She's not my slave, I can't just turn her over to you."

"Was you joking when you asked to see the title to my Firebird?" Virgil asked coldly.

"That didn't mean anything."

"Where we come from, a bet's a bet. We can do this the honest way and you don't get hurt, or we can do it the hard way."

Darren's face tightened. He clenched his fists. "Bring it on, hillbilly."

Virgil smirked. Lester put two fingers in his mouth and let out an ear-splitting whistle. From the bar, two men stood and started to come their way. They were older, both big and round-shouldered, thick arms.

Meredith figured they had a few seconds, no more, to reach the side door before the reinforcements arrived. Darren could lower his shoulder, knock Virgil into Lester and clear a path. If they moved now!

"Darren, let's go!" She grabbed his wrist, ready to hang on for dear life.

"I'm sorry, Meri," he said, yanking his arm free. Head down, he rammed Lester with lowered shoulder, slamming him to the floor. Virgil tried to grab Darren's arm but he shook him off, plowed straight through a clot of women, knocking one to the ground. The two men from the bar charged toward Darren.

"You BAAA-STARD!" Meredith's bellow halted all conversations mid-sentence. Even the band stopped playing. Everyone turned their heads to gape at Meredith, who stood in the passageway, arms in the air, a slim pretty young woman in a fitted tee and shorts, sun-streaked brown hair pulled back into a ponytail. Then their heads swiveled to watch a broad-shouldered man sprint through the side door.

"Well, I sure hope that wasn't directed at *me*," the band singer quipped. Laughter rippled through the bar. A few patrons gave Meredith lingering, curious looks; most resumed talking, drinking, smoking, flirting. The band went back to their cover of "Please Stay Tuned."

One of Virgil's friends ticked his head toward the door. *Go after him?* Virgil shook his head. They nodded and returned to the bar.

Meredith strode over to Lester, who was now on his knees, grimacing as he started to stand. She extended a hand.

"Sorry about that. You hurt?"

"Ahh, I'll be fine. Your old man's a bull, though, I'll give him that."

"*Ex*-old man, thanks to you." Meredith was all smiles as she hugged Lester and then Virgil, kissing them both on the cheek.

"Happy to help," Virgil said. "Gotta say, we had to have Filbert tell us twice what you wanted to do."

"I know, sorry. I tried to keep this hustle simple."

"Once we understood it through and through, we knew we could do it."

Through and through. Good phrase, Meredith thought. As in, she was through with Darren. For a short time, she had hoped he would get over whatever was eating him, get back to being the fun-loving, pool-sharking man she'd fallen in with. But when he got physical—uh-uh, no way she was giving him another chance. While he slept off his beer and whiskey one night in Canton, she snuck out to the hotel lobby and called her Uncle Filbert at his pool hall in Lexington, where she had met Lester and Virgil. Before she left town for good, the three of them had played something like a thousand games of cut-throat together. She had heard they'd ended up in Chicago. *Know how to get ahold of them?* Meredith had asked Filbert. *'Spect I can do that*, he had answered. Feeding dime after dime into the payphone for the long-distance call, she had outlined her plan, Filbert repeating each step back to her to make sure he understood. *All set*, he told her the following night when she snuck out for another call. *Saturday night, Carol's Pub in Uptown—they'll be there.*

"Boy, you sure can act, Meredith," Lester now said, rubbing his chest where Darren had butted him. "S'like you'd never seen us before."

"You boys did pretty good yourselves."

"How'd you know he'd go for my car?" Virgil asked.

"On our way here, I told him the transmission on his Nova felt off. I'd called ahead to a garage, told the mechanic I'd give him twenty bucks to pop the hood and tell us we needed two-hundred-eighty-two bucks to fix it."

Virgil chortled. "So there's nothing wrong with his car?"

"Nope, not a lick."

"Too bad he got away with it."

"Did he?" Meredith grinned as she pulled Darren's key ring from her shorts pocket.

Both men gaped. "How'd you do that?" Lester asked.

"Remember when I jumped on him after Virgil won, how I wrapped myself around him? When he let me down, I picked his pockets."

Virgil nodded admiringly but Lester looked worried.

"Should we be worried about him coming back?"

Meredith firmly shook her head. "After ditching me like that? He'll slink off, find some place to hustle a stake to get out of town. And I'll never have to see him again."

"What'd he do to you?" Lester said.

She let her stoic expression serve as reply; Lester didn't press.

"Gotta say, I was frettin' a bit over playing nine ball," Virgil said. "But he took the bait just like you said he would, breaking the rack wide open."

"That's his weakness," Meredith said. "No patience. Hey, here's your bread back." She counted off two-hundred dollars and pressed them into Virgil's hand.

"You don't gotta do that," he protested awkwardly.

"Take it. I pulled it outta his pocket when I snagged the keys."

He dipped his chin and accepted the cash. "So what's next, Meredith? You wanna stick around a few days, get to know Chicago?"

Why not? She'd been so focused on running the hustle to rid herself of Darren, she hadn't thought about what came next.

"I'd like that, sure," she answered.

"You can stay with my sister."

"That sounds great."

"Maybe you can teach us a thing or too," Lester said.

"You bet." Meredith looked at the beat-up, raggedy, sorry-ass table that had aided her liberation. "S'long as it's not here."

THE TROUBLE WITH SPIDERS

K.L. Abrahamson

Every morning I check my slippers for spiders. I throw off the covers, fumble for my glasses and, with my feet chilling on the cold linoleum floor, check that spiders didn't nest in my slippers overnight. There is nothing worse than feeling spidery legs thrashing against your toes or that !POP! as their small round bodies explode.

It is such a mess getting their guts out of faux fleece.

I don't hate spiders. I respect the orderliness of their lives and the perfect webs between branches or in the tall grass. The dew on the silken strands glistens jewel-like in the morning sun.

But there is something horrible about the motionless way spiders wait and then leap on the unsuspecting bee or butterfly drawn in by that morning beauty, only to be sucked dry by the spider.

I don't like the way the prey jerks and trembles as the spider wraps them in silk. I hate to see the suffering.

That's why I usually smash those beautiful webs with a rock.

Her name was Emelia-Jean and she lived downstairs from me in the Imperial Apartments, an ancient, brick and wood, fire-trap building on the east side of the city. In the fall, when she moved in, it was the talk of the fifteen of us who already lived there. Emelia-Jean of the long gray hair that she wore twisted back in a perfect bun, her petite figure draped in a gray t-shirt and old-fashioned, frayed bell-bottoms with flowers embroidered around the hem. When I almost plowed into her going down the stairs from my third-floor walk-up, she gave me that wide smile of hers that erased any lines on her face and made me acutely aware of my wrinkles, my bowl-cut, graying brown hair and the creases in my shiny gabardine interview suit.

"I'm so sorry!" I said and caught her thin wrist to steady her. "Are you looking for someone?"

"Nope," she said juggling a small box that still looked too large for her to manage. "I'm your new neighbor. Emelia-Jean Newman. I'm moving into 203."

"Samantha Cooper," I said. "Sam around here. You're moving just downstairs from me. Let me give you a hand." I leaned my photography portfolio against the wall and helped her with the box. I helped with five more, bringing them up from her car and introducing her to other residents. Then I noticed the time. I had an appointment for a possible commercial photography job. By the time I found my portfolio again, I had brought in six other Imperial residents to help Emelia-Jean, and I was hopelessly late and considerably more dusty.

"Thank you so much," she said as I rushed to leave. "It looks like you're a real leader here."

"I just know everybody." I shrugged and ran.

I didn't get the job and by the time I got home, the Imperial Apartments were changed forever. Emelia-Jean had moved in and all the residents had helped her.

I think it was part of her plan.

It started with Stuart.

Stuart Blackman was a sixty-plus-year-old who lived on the first floor. A semi-retired saxophonist, he subsisted on a government pension and what he made busking outside the liquor store. He was a tall, balding drink of water with wide-set ears and a protruding nose that probably served him well when playing, and play sweetly he did. When his saxophone wasn't in his hands he acted like he'd lost a limb.

Without his saxophone he bumbled around. The first time I met him he asked whether my daughter had left me or I'd deserted her. The awkwardness came when I told him she'd died. But he'd been kind to me when I moved in after my divorce. He'd invited me for coffee and had come to my place for tea. He'd played me songs when I was so tired I thought maybe living was beyond me. That man's saxophone would purr and rumble and cry in his hands. He'd play me everything but Celine Dion, because we'd quickly established that I couldn't abide that chanteuse's music. He'd also been one of the people I introduced to Emelia-Jean and spent the day helping her move in.

I worried a little about his awkward questions, but things seemed okay. Stuart followed her around like a puppy and was at her beck and call. I noticed the coffee invitations came less often, but that was okay too. I was too busy. I had to hustle as a freelance photographer.

But then I didn't see Stuart on the stairs. I didn't see him busking at the liquor store either. When I went to his apartment, through the closed door all he said was "Go away."

They found him a few weeks later. He'd died from a sleeping pill overdose though he had no prescription for them.

The coroner ruled death by misadventure—an accident—but I wasn't so sure.

I mean, sure the Imperial Apartments had their fair share of sudden deaths, but where did he get the pills from and what happened that he needed to take them?

I worried that I hadn't been there for Stuart and, frankly, it kept me up at night. Fourteen of us from the apartments kicked in funds to get him a proper funeral. Only Emelia-Jean didn't.

"I barely knew him," she said when I asked her to contribute. It was six months after we welcomed her.

Carol Joe was a single mother of two little girls with a third baby on the way. There were no fathers in the picture and if Carol knew who they were, she wasn't saying. But live and let live, I used to say, so Carol and I were friends. She lived on the first floor, but I'd watch the girls sometimes during the day and had permission to use them as models. I also watched them at night when Carol needed to sow some wild oats. I made it like a camping adventure for the girls. We'd build a tent in a corner of the living room and I'd spread couch cushions for them to sleep on. It worked out fine until Emelia-Jean moved in.

I ran into Carol and the girls a number of times after Emelia-Jean moved in. The girls always gave Aunty Sam a big hug and asked when they could stay with me again. Carol always looked embarrassed, apologized for all the times she'd left the girls with me and led them up to the second floor.

Everyone in the building knew where they were going. Children's tunes trilled from Emelia-Jean's stereo and we heard children's laughter. I have to say it hurt and I missed them.

Then one day Children's Services showed up and apprehended Carol's children. According to the Imperial's rumors, Emelia-Jean had called them because Carol 'deserted them on her doorstep daily and had previously left them in the care of someone suspect'—namely me.

"Suspect how?" I demanded when I called Children's Services in Carol's defense. I was seated at my small kitchen table. Outside, the trees were in Spring bloom but across from me sat a tearful Carol.

"Aren't you a photographer?" asked the too-careful voice at the end of the phone. The voice reminded me of caramel—too thick to swallow.

"What does my photography have to do with anything?"

"Did you take pictures of the children?"

"I had Carol's permission."

"What kind of images, Ms. Cooper?" The smooth caramel voice reached through the phone and grabbed me by the throat.

"Pictures of them playing. Sisters hugging?"

"In the bath together?"

"Well, yes. But those photos were for Carol. The girls were adorable in the soap suds."

"Hmm-hmm."

I came up off my chair. "Just one darn minute. Did someone say I did something wrong with those children? I would never hurt Daisy and Glory!"

"You have to understand. We're responsible for ensuring those children are safe."

I hung up. "Someone's suggested I was taking inappropriate photos of the girls. Who would think such a thing?"

Carol wouldn't look at me, and her veil of black hair screened her face. "I ... Emelia-Jean said I needed to be careful ... I never believed, but ..." She raised a teary gaze to me. "Why would she say it, if it wasn't true? Why would she say I abandoned my girls?"

Her hands slid protectively over her rounded stomach. I slumped in my chair. "How the heck should I know?"

I didn't know what to do. Protest my innocence, sure, but didn't pornographers do that too? Besides, protesting to the authorities had only made me look more guilty. But why would Emelia-Jean target me? I'd only welcomed her to the building.

I thought of Stuart and looked at Carol. "You need to protect yourself, Carol." I did too.

"I'm going to tell her off. I'm going to make her tell the truth," Carol said with more spine than she'd ever shown. She stood and marched out my door.

I didn't see her for a few days. The Imperial seemed awash in shadows without the giggles of Carol's girls.

A week later I arrived home to find ambulances and police at the Imperial's door. Carol had fallen down the third-floor stairs. Of course she lost the baby. I visited her in the hospital, but the fall had done more than make her miscarry—it stole her will to live. When I tried to hold her hand and promised I'd help her get her girls back, she simply rolled away from me.

When I spoke to the nurses about my concern, they advised me that her other friend was caring for Carol's affairs. By their description, it was Emelia-Jean.

Carol never returned to the Imperial. A couple of guys removed her stuff and I never saw her girls again. Over the summer, I quietly spoke to my neighbors on the third floor, but no one could give me a reason why she'd even been on the floor—unless she was trying to reach me.

Had someone stopped her?

It had to be Emelia-Jean. If Carol had confronted her. But surely Emelia-Jean wouldn't shove a pregnant woman down the stairs. That was too horrific to imagine.

But there had been Stuart and there had been the removal of Carol's children ...

I needed to know more about this woman.

I'm no investigator, but I thought talking to her previous neighbors might tell me something. So I visited Charlie Vine, our officious little building manager. I figured he'd know where she'd come from.

Charlie lived in a small, ground-floor suite that gave out onto the lane behind the Imperial. Charlie had his own door to the lane and small grilled windows that were overgrown with every kind of houseplant you could imagine. When I knocked on his door, at first I didn't think he was home. I hugged myself for warmth in the cool fall wind with leaves and discarded paper rattling along the building walls. The air smelled of garbage from the dumpster ten feet away. It was hard to imagine that Emelia-Jean had lived in the Imperial a full year.

I knocked again.

"I'm coming. Don't get your britches in a knot." The door locks rattled and the door pulled open.

Charlie blinked out at me. He was an owl-eyed man of about five-foot-seven, only an inch shorter than me, but I always felt big because he was so rail thin. His bulging eyes and heavy brows made him look surprised, but today he looked at me as if I was a stranger.

"Charlie. Hi. Can I talk to you a minute?"

"Uhh. I was just eating." He looked up and down the lane and then studied his shoes.

"Charlie. It's me, Sam. Remember? I helped you out dealing with Mr. McCann when he needed to go into the home. I called the ambulance when you fell and broke your leg."

"Yeah. Yeah." He stepped aside to let me in.

Going into Charlie's place was like stepping into a dark green liquid. The small windows were enveloped with plants starving for light, so overlong fronds, stems, leaves and vines all trailed around the room as they searched for a light source. Their overly thin owner had the same starved look, but maybe it was for attention.

He led me into the living room with its worn couch and wall-mounted state-of-the-art television. The kitchen table in the corner was bare. So much for his story about eating.

He turned to face me.

"We haven't talked in a while," I said feeling uncomfortable with how this was going. "But I'm concerned with what's happened in the building. First Stuart and now Carol."

His brows twitched, but he said nothing. I began to doubt what I was doing here.

"Do—do you think there could be any connection?" I finished lamely. I just couldn't bring up Emelia-Jean.

"What are you talking about?"

"Well … can you think of anything that's changed in the Imperial? Friends that they had in common …"

His gaze met mine and I swear he knew where I was going.

"Like you?" he asked, his expression unfriendly.

"Me? Of course they knew me. Everyone knows me."

He shook his head. "Everyone knows you cozied up to Stuart and Carol and those little girls."

All the blood ran from my head. I felt stunned and unsteady and grabbed the wall for balance. Charlie jerked back as if I threatened him.

"What are you saying? I knew them just like everyone."

Charlie shook his head.

"Are people talking about me?"

He wouldn't meet my gaze.

"Charlie, you've known me five years. Have I ever given you a lick of trouble?"

A slight shake of head.

"Then who's talking about me? What are they saying?"

He glanced up at me. "I don't like spreading rumors."

"Neither do I," I said with a sigh. "Don't I deserve to know what's being said behind my back?"

He licked his thin lips and looked around as if trying to find an escape, but finally he looked at me squarely. "People say that you and Stuart were lovers and you dumped him. That's why he killed himself." He swallowed. "And that you took pictures of Carol's girls."

"Jeezus." I was going to be sick. I needed to sit down.

Instead I swallowed the nausea back. "None of it's true."

No nod. No shake of head. Nothing.

I took a deep breath. "Can I ask who made these pronouncements about me?"

Another lick of lips. "It was more an observation. Someone saw things clearly. Like with new eyes."

"Aah," I said and stood there inhaling the scent of wet earth and green, trying to figure out what to do. What to say. "Emelia-Jean, was it." It wasn't a question. I knew.

"Listen, I don't need trouble between tenants." He held up his hands as if to placate me, but being placated wasn't what was on my mind.

I could have killed the woman.

"Where did she come from? The city or one of the suburbs?"

His owl eyes bulged at the change of conversational trajectory. Shuffling away he sank down on his couch, a palm frond falling shawl-like over his shoulder.

"The city. She had an apartment on the West Side. Was renovicted like everyone else in the building. She saw it coming and had already found this place. The Oceanview." He smiled as if he'd scored a win by attracting someone from such a high rent building.

Which begged the question of why anyone who could afford the Oceanview was renting in the Imperial. The Imperial is clean and there are no rats, but that was about all there was to recommend a fifty-year-old three-story walk-up building with creaking floors, drafts and constantly weeping windows. Charlie, of course, didn't seem to get this.

After thanking him and leaving, I went for a walk to calm my boiling blood. Then I climbed on a bus bound for the west side of Vancouver. My phone told me the Oceanview was on Cornwall Avenue.

The sun felt distant, its weak light unable to dispel the chill off the ocean. Waves crashed on the beach across the road as I stood in front of a gleaming, fifteen-story condo complex. The place didn't look like it needed renovations at all.

I buzzed the manager, but he refused to speak to me when asked about a previous tenant. So I decided to loiter outside the building's front door. Sure enough, an elderly woman dragging a rickety grocery trolley turned in from the street toward the glass front door.

"Excuse me," I said. "I wonder whether you could help me?"

She was an elegant woman with smile lines etching her face. She had long-fingered hands with fine fingernails and three diamond rings. She wore a camel-colored coat and a rose-colored scarf and her gray hair was coiled up in a lovely chignon.

She straightened and raked me with a sharp blue gaze, her hand already holding her keys. "If you're selling, I'm not buying."

And wouldn't suffer fools … Well, in for a penny …

"I'm trying to gather information about a previous tenant. This person moved into my building and since then some issues have arisen."

The woman's gaze narrowed. "Are you talking about noise infractions and smoking in the hallways?"

I shook my head.

She looked across at the beach and sighed. "Will this never end? I thought we were rid of her."

"Emelia-Jean," I said.

She nodded, her gaze never leaving the heaving water and the sailboats racing in front of the wind.

"Can you tell me what happened here? Where I live there's been a death and a woman has had her children apprehended." I didn't mention the accusations against me.

She gave a small nod and shivered. A car passed in the street, stirring the leaves along the curb. "That's about right. That's how it started here too. Then things got worse until we were her servants. A group of us finally went to the owner and asked for the renoviction to get her to leave. We're all paying increased rents now, but at least we can live our own lives."

"Can you tell me what went on?" I held out my hand. "I'm Samantha Cooper."

She glanced at my hand and then at my face. Her own face paled and fear bloomed in her eyes. Then she shook her head. "That's how she weaseled her way into our lives. All friendly like you are. How do I know she didn't send you? That she just wants to cause more trouble. Please don't hurt us again. Please."

Her hands shook as she fumbled her keys. She struggled with the door against the wind. In the end I opened it for her. She entered and firmly shut the door in my face. I had my confirmation.

I didn't need to speak to anyone else, but I waited and spoke to an older gentleman who was even less forthcoming. Then a committee of ten residents showed up from inside the building.

"This is your only warning. Please leave the premises or we'll be forced to call the police," said their elderly male spokesperson through the half-open door.

Even through the glass I could see the fear glazing their eyes. Some of the women held hands like the victims rescued from concentration camps.

"I'm sorry I've frightened you. I'm trying to stop bad things from happening in my building."

"If you have her in your building, I wish you good luck." The door pulled shut and they stood there waiting.

I turned and left.

It was almost as if she knew what I'd done. Perhaps Charlie told her I'd asked about her, or maybe someone at the Oceanview told her I visited, but the attacks on me turned more direct. Emelia-Jean knew I couldn't be manipulated like many of the other tenants, but she focused her attention on me.

That was when the music started.

I was processing images on my computer, trying to create something new and wonderful out of images that were simply old and clichéd. I was looking for inspiration and opened the window to lean out to clear my head in the weak fall sunlight.

From the open window downstairs came the unmistakable opening strains of the theme from 'Titanic.'

Now I hate Celine Dion's music, but I'll still defend everyone's right to play what they like, however that particular song makes my skin crawl. When the movie came out, I practically overdosed on the song's treacly, over-sweet message. I'd loved. I'd married. I'd been burned and I was a realist. The Titanic kind of love simply didn't exist for most people. Love someone, but don't expect it to turn into a Hollywood movie. Too many people did.

So I'd avoided the song and people who liked me didn't play it when I was around. I pulled in my head and returned to my computer, leaving the window barely cracked open. The song would end.

Or so I thought.

When the song finished, it started again and it was louder. I closed my window. Surely no one could listen to that song a third time in a row.

The song ended and started again.

At the computer I tried not to listen.

The fourth time the song repeated I paced around the room. This was no accident. Someone had told Emelia-Jean about my abhorrence.

I tried to keep working, but I was being assaulted by sound. I finally packed up my laptop and went out. When I returned late that afternoon, the music started again and played late into the night.

Followed by the same thing the next day.

And the next.

And the next.

And the next.

At first, the walls of the apartment were my defense. It was fall, so I didn't need my windows open. But the music seemed to seep through the old wooden floorboards and sneak up through the walls. Even sound cancelling headphones didn't work. Celine's quavering voice vibrated up through the floor until everything I owned was sodden with her cries. I was drowning in it. Until *my* heart couldn't go on any longer.

Until I had to do something. Emelia-Jean had moved in and was taking root, just like she'd once done at the Oceanview. I'd already run into arthritic, eighty-three-year-old Sophie from the first floor lugging groceries to the second floor for Emelia-Jean.

I decided to pay her a visit.

She didn't look surprised to see me.

"Samantha. To what do I owe this pleasure?" she said with a too-smug smile. She was wearing tie-dye leggings and a navy tunic that covered half of her skinny thighs. Her long hair hung loose around her shoulders like one of those trippy dancers from the Woodstock festival. She draped one arm casually across her doorway to block any entry, not that I wanted to go in. Celine's trills spilled out the door around her.

"You need to stop," I said, feeling huge and ungainly next to this woman, but that was part of her intimidation.

She shook her head as if she didn't understand. "Enlighten me, please? What are you talking about?"

"The music. The rumors. Everything."

She frowned prettily. "I'm sorry. Are you suggesting I'm not allowed to enjoy music in my home?"

I wasn't suggesting that, but it would sound that way no matter what I said. "You've been playing the same song over and over for a week. Play something else."

She glanced up and down the hallway. "No one else is complaining."

"Everyone else is too scared to." Damn. I hadn't meant to tell her what I knew.

"Really? Maybe we should have this conversation inside."

She undraped her arm and motioned me into the swelling music.

Her place was different than the day she moved in. I followed her into the living room with her overstuffed red couch and large TV on the wall. A faux fireplace looked suspiciously like the one Stuart had had in his apartment. An ornately carved floral wall-plaque reminded me of one I'd admired in Sophie's apartment. Next to the couch sat an embroidered footstool that had belonged to another resident's dear-departed husband. Stacks of books and magazines that I suspected she'd mined from the resident bookworms filled the floor.

I felt sick to my stomach at the things she had stripped away from my friends. These things. Carol's children. Stuart's life.

My reputation seemed like nothing, but now she'd stolen the peace of my home. I couldn't even see Bylaws doing something given I was the only complainant.

She crossed the room to the CD player. A stack of un-cased CDs sat on the top.

She turned to me, her arms crossed over her chest. "So what are you going to do about it?" she asked as Celine belted out about opening a door. "Because from where I stand there's nothing you can do to make me stop. You're the only one complaining and everyone knows you're a troublemaker and a perv."

Her words ran over me like another stanza of Celine's song. Actually, her voice helped dispel some of the sticky glue the music seemed to form in my brain.

"I guess I have you to thank for that too, Emelia-Jean."

She shrugged. "When I moved in everyone I talked to said what a powerhouse you were. You got the owners to fix the furnace. You got front door locks replaced. Everyone looked to you if something needed doing. You probably enjoyed the adulation. All gone now that they know the truth though."

"Your truth, maybe." I stepped over a pile of books toward her. "So you had to undermine me, so you could control them just like you did at the Oceanview. You spun your web around these people just like you did there."

"Bunch of ingrates," she snarled.

"How long do you think you can take advantage here before these folks force you to move along?"

She shrugged. "Long enough to milk them of the best of what they have." She motioned around the room. "But you won't care because you'll be long gone."

I stepped up to her as the music crescendoed and began again. "I'm not leaving." I reached around her to the stereo and clicked the eject button. The CD ejected smoothly and I pulled it out. Quiet descended and I felt like I could breathe again.

"What the fuck do you think you're doing? That's my CD. My music."

She made a grab for the CD but I held it up, just out of her reach.

"You might intimidate some people, but you don't intimidate me," I said as I stepped back, still clutching the CD.

She lunged, grabbed me by the waist and spun me around so that we crashed into the TV. In the tangle of books, my feet were trapped and I went down with a crash right next to the fireplace, Emelia-Jean with me. She pried at my fingers around the CD.

"Jeezus, woman! Are you insane?" I shoved her off and tossed the CD onto the couch.

She dove for it, her eyes wild. "This is my stuff. My CD. Did you know that everyone in this building has copies of the Titanic song? Those are all their CDs there." She motioned at the stack of uncased CDs on the stereo. "Everyone's been afraid to play the damned song because of you. Did you know? You and me—we're not that different."

I wanted to slap that smug smile off her face. "I don't take people's stuff. I don't make them work for me."

"Really? It sounded like that the day I moved in. You rounded up everyone you could and got them working to help me."

"But—that was different. We were helping a new neighbor."

She just returned to the CD player and slid in the CD. The opening strains of Titanic filled the room and something slipped in my brain, because I couldn't go on and on.

Not like this.

It took two strides to cross the room and one huge shove to send her crashing back against her stereo. The shelf unit shuddered and collapsed. Her head crashed against the wall. CDs flew up in a hailstorm around her.

The stereo slid to the floor and the music stopped and so, apparently, did Emily-Jean in a heap among the uncased CDs. I went to her side as a red stream pumped from her neck. One of the broken CD's caught her there. It was sharp. I tried to stop the bleeding while I dialled 911.

All to no avail. Emily died amid the wreckage of the Titanic theme song.

The police wanted to charge me with murder for Emelia-Jean's death, but the prosecutor thought better of it once they took a look at her past. The people of Oceanview finally spoke out and it seemed some Imperial residents did too. I was charged with manslaughter, but my lawyer thinks I'll likely get off with probation. That I can do.

So the music has stopped and I still live in the Imperial Apartments. The other residents are talking to me again, but I notice a twitch in them every time I ask for anything—almost as if they're afraid. Which brings me back to spiders.

I still check my slippers for them every morning, but I haven't seen one in my apartment for a very long time.

Did I mention that two spiders in the same web will usually battle to the death?

A CRACK IN THE SIDEWALK

Michael Biehl

It was because of the Willevers, who lived across the street from my family in 1963, that I learned at the age of ten just how unstable and twisted adult life can be. It was because of them that I knew that even in a seemingly safe, affluent, all-American suburb, outwardly normal families sometimes teeter on the precipice of self-inflicted calamity. Because of them, I found out at an early age what a dead body looked like. A fresh one.

My home town of Oak Hills, Minnesota boasted a new village park with a swimming pool, tennis courts, and most importantly by far, two baseball diamonds. For me and my buddies, summer vacation and baseball were synonymous. We didn't much care for Little League, with all of the pressure and self-consciousness inflicted on us by adult managers, umpires, and parents constantly monitoring and fussing, taking all of the fun out of it.

"Grown-ups are stupid," said my best friend, Jeremy. "They ruin everything."

It was thanks to Jeremy that we did not need grown-ups to organize baseball games that were infinitely more fun than Little League. A precocious, self-reliant, red-headed Wunderkind who was never more serious than when he played ball, Jeremy got on the phone and pulled us all together at the village park three afternoons a week. He and I tossed a bat, hands-upped with no topsies, chose sides, took the field, and played all afternoon, razzing and ribbing each other the whole time. We took occasional breaks to wrestle, throw water balloons, or chase down the ice cream truck.

In my memory of those glorious games, I'm always happily in center field, the sun is always shining, my team is always winning, I never make an error, and time does not exist. There will always be another inning, another game, another sunny afternoon, another summer vacation, forever.

When we weren't playing baseball, Jeremy and I were often laughing at dirty jokes, practical jokes, *Mad* magazine, or our own waggish remarks about how stupid grown-ups were. We rode our bikes all over town, getting into the sort of minor mischief ten-year-old boys will, if unsupervised, like playing with firecrackers and slingshots, and putting pennies on the railroad tracks. It was a gas. Most of the time, our parents didn't know where we were, or what we were doing. The only restriction imposed on me was that I had to be home in time for dinner.

If a game was close and I was having a good day at the plate, I was prone to losing track of the time and missing dinner entirely. When I did, my father never said a word, because in order to impose discipline he would have had to interrupt his post-prandial tippling. It fell to my mother to be the disciplinarian. Her technique was limited to biting sarcasm, which stung like pineapple juice on a canker sore.

One hot, cloudless afternoon in mid-July, a three-run tie went into extra innings, and not only did I miss dinner, I had to pump my bike pedals like I was in the *Tour de France* to make it home before sunset. I was sure I was in for a sarcastic keel-hauling worthy of Don Rickles.

When I got home, an ambulance blocked the driveway, which shot a pang of fear through my chest. Did my father have a heart attack? My parents often talked about having heart attacks. So often, in fact, that I sometimes thought *I* was having a heart attack.

I was relieved to see my parents standing on the front walk, talking to the neighbors from across the street, Joan and Tom Willever. Joan, a petite brunette, wore pedal pushers and a bare midriff blouse. She had a face that gave me the same funny feeling inside that I got when I looked at a cute ten year-old girl. Tom was tall and lanky, with a crew cut and a tattoo on his forearm. From my parents' stiff bodies and grim faces, I sensed something peculiar and deadly serious was afoot.

"That's it, right *there*," said Tom in a loud, commanding tone. He jabbed his index finger at the sidewalk. "That crack is pitched up almost two inches. Joan tripped on that."

My mother glared at my father, her face full of anxiety and agitation. My father's face was flushed.

"No, Tom, that's not where she fell," said my father. "She fell stepping off the front door step. I think the sun got in her eyes."

I dropped my bike on the front lawn. Blood ran from Mrs. Willever's left knee. She had skinned it pretty severely, but I'd had worse skinned knees that my mother treated with Mercurochrome and a Band-Aid.

An ambulance? Weird.

My mother spotted me, and said, "Andy, go in the house right now. Make yourself a peanut butter sandwich." Not a word about my inexcusable tardiness.

I went into the house, a red brick Colonial, and peeked out the window at my parents and the neighbors, all of them grim-faced, inflamed, pointing fingers, and smoking cigarettes. Mrs. Willever limped to the ambulance, looking pathetic and adorable. Tom shouted something about a hazardous condition, negligence, and a lawsuit. My parents slinked into the house, which was baking hot inside.

"She wasn't anywhere near that crack," said my father. "Tom Willever is full of crap."

"We'll talk about it later," said my mother. "After Andy's asleep."

There was no way I was going to sleep after that teaser. I cracked my bedroom door open an inch. They tried to cover their conversation with *The Tonight Show*, but I could still hear a lot of it.

"We don't have any insurance for this, do we, Harry?" Acid in her voice.

"He's not going to sue us over a skinned knee, Helen."

"Oh, he's going to sue us all right, but not over a skinned knee."

"What do you mean?"

After a long pause, my mother growled, "What was Joan Willever doing in the house?"

"She dropped by for a visit. A neighborly visit."

"When she could see my station wagon wasn't in the garage."

"The poor woman needed to talk to someone. That husband of hers is a beast."

"Oh, aren't you gallant. Did *he* smear her lipstick? You both reek of gin. You're lucky he didn't break your nose."

"He's a pinhead. How ridiculous, calling an ambulance. I should sue *him*. For trespass."

"Oh yeah, a lot of tough talk."

"That shed in his backyard violates the village ordinances. I should report him."

"Big, tough man."

After that night, an icy silence settled on our home, until a letter came in the mail that triggered an explosion of ominous warnings and accusations. My mother was so furious she brandished the letter at me, to show me what dire straits my father had sailed us into. The letter, from a lawyer representing the Willevers, threatened a lawsuit for $35,000 for Mrs. Willever's injury. The same day it arrived, two men in suits and ties came to take photographs of the crack in the front walk, with a ruler standing on end to show how high up the crack was pitched.

My mother sat me down at our tubular metal and Formica kitchen table, and explained to me in somber tones that our lives were about to change. The crack in the sidewalk meant we were negligent. $35,000 was more than our equity in the house, whatever that meant, and more than my father made at his job at the power company in three years. We had no insurance. We were going to have to sell the house, and move out of Oak Hills, to an apartment. I had no inkling that she may have been exaggerating or panicking. My mother said it, I thought it must be true. I hopped on my bike and rode to Jeremy's house at breakneck speed.

I stood at his screen door and told him what had happened, and that my family might have to move away. He took it hard.

"Grown-ups are so *stupid!*" he yelled, and ran through his house, screaming. He slammed the door to his bedroom, presumably to pout, and didn't come out. He recovered enough to organize a ballgame the next day, but a pall hung over everything we did for the rest of July.

In August, the Willever's lawyer served my parents with the lawsuit. Now it was $45,000.

"What are you going to do about this, Harry?" said my mother. "You gonna sit there guzzling gin while Tom Willever ruins our lives?"

"That son-of-a-bitch will rue the day."

"Yeah, big talk. You're scared to death of Tom."

"What do you expect me to do, Helen? Engage in fisticuffs with an ex-Marine ten years younger than me?"

"No. I *expect* you to sit on your behind and flap your jaw while everything we have goes down the drain."

"Helen, I could use a little moral support right now."

"Call Joan. Maybe *she'll* give you some."

"Please, dear."

"Get rid of the damn lawsuit, Harry. If I have to move my son to an apartment in the city, you won't be moving there with us."

The dog days of August dragged on, parching and menacing, while the atmosphere in our house reeked of hostility and dread. My parent's conversation dwelt on bewildering, fanciful strategies to fabricate money to settle the lawsuit, occasionally punctuated by cutting remarks about the Willevers, my father's directed at Tom, my mother's directed at "that floozy." My mother didn't bother to take me to the store to shop for back-to-school stuff, since where I would be in school that year, and what we could afford, were up in the air due to the lawsuit. My father brooded and drank more than usual. He began to look haggard all the time.

As often happens in Minnesota, a cold day swept in from Canada by surprise in the heart of August, breaking the heat, but also warning of the impending long, stern winter ahead. I felt so sad out in center field, realizing that summer would soon be over, and I might not be back next season. I heard the sound of sirens in the distance, which sounded to me like a dire omen.

My team held a two-run lead in the ninth, with two runners on and one out, when Jeremy hit a short fly to center that looked like it would drop and score two runs. I stretched out to attempt a shoe-string catch, and came up with the ball in the web of my glove. I threw to second, doubling off Todd Pfeiffer, who had not tagged up, to end the game. Possibly.

"He short-hopped it!" yelled Todd, the tying run, standing on third. "I saw it hit the ground."

We had no umpires, so disputes of this nature were a regular part of the game. My guys would all insist I caught it cleanly, Jeremy's teammates would back Todd. Evidence of dubious validity would be loudly asserted, and either one side would yield, or we'd play a do-over. This dispute was a big deal, because the game was on the line, and there wasn't enough afternoon left to play another.

The rhubarb ended when Jeremy did something completely unprecedented.

"Andy caught it on the fly," he said. "I saw it clearly."

The authority of a team captain backing a disputed call that favored the opposing team could not be questioned. All deferred to Jeremy's awe-inspiring display of self-sacrificial integrity, including me, even though I thought I short-hopped it.

"Nice catch, buddy," he said, as I mounted my bike for the ride home. "That was worthy of Willie Mays. See you tomorrow." Jeremy knew Willie Mays was my idol.

Once again, when I got home I saw an ambulance. This one was parked in the street with its lights flashing. Two squad cars, also with flashing lights, generated an atmosphere of frenzy and chaos. Neighbors milled about in the street. Policemen and paramedics in uniforms bustled to and fro. My parents stood on the front walk, smoking cigarettes.

"What's going on?" I said.

"Tom Willever's been injured," said my father. "In his tool shed. They're bringing him out now."

Two paramedics bore Tom on a stretcher from the tool shed in his backyard to the waiting ambulance. Policemen waved the cluster of gawking neighbors back, to clear the way. I rolled down our driveway on my bike until I was about ten feet from the ambulance. As they loaded him in, I got a good look. Tom flopped about on the stretcher like a string of dead fish. His right arm dangled off the stretcher, misshapen and black as soot. Our next door neighbor, Mrs. Martino, stood in the Willevers' driveway, with her arm around Joan Willever, who held her face in her hands, and trembled.

Mr. Martino, an avuncular, white-haired man who smoked a pipe, had a blunt way of talking to me that I liked, because he wasn't condescending, like most grown-ups.

"What happened?" I said.

"He electrocuted himself in his tool shed," said Mr. Martino. He puffed his pipe. "Damn fool."

"How could that happen?"

"Don't know yet. Could have been that twenty-year-old Coleman table saw. That thing was never properly grounded. It gives you a little shock every time you touch it. They'll figure it out."

"Is Mr. Willever going to be okay?"

"I'm afraid not, Andy. If he had any chance at all, they'd have got him into that ambulance a lot faster."

I looked at Mrs. Martino trying to comfort Joan Willever. I felt achingly sad. "What's going to happen to Mrs. Willever?"

"Poor woman. If it was the table saw, the Coleman Tool Company will have to pay a lot of money. The Willevers are suers." He took a few more puffs. "I guess you know that."

For the first time in over a month, that night my parents talked to each other over dinner in an animated, and somewhat friendly manner. They finally had something to talk about other than whether they could get enough on a second mortgage to settle the lawsuit, or whether Joan Willever was a "loose woman."

"I always said Tom had dangerous equipment in that tool shed," said my father. "And he tells me *my* sidewalk is a hazard."

"Andy, you see now why I told you and your friends to stay away from that shed," said my mother.

"The village ordinances prohibit outbuildings. It's an attractive nuisance. I should have reported him."

"How careless, to electrocute yourself in this day and age. You'd think people would know better."

"You'd be surprised how many reports we get at the power company about accidental electrocutions. Idiots."

Eventually, they got around to the crux of the matter.

"Do you think Joan will drop the lawsuit now?" said my mother.

My father smiled. "I'm sure she will. She never wanted to pretend that she had a serious knee injury in the first place. Now, she's got a wrongful death claim that's actually worth something. With Tom's veterans' life insurance, she's all set."

"Did you see her walking in the driveway with Donna Martino? What happened to the limp? What a faker."

"Tom forced her to do that. She's better off without that jerk."

If I was disturbed by my parent's display of *schadenfreude,* it was obscured by the relief I felt hearing them enjoy a conversation for a change. I eavesdropped again that night, because it gave me a rare feeling of security to hear my parents in cahoots.

"Did you see his arm?" said my mother. "Jesus. He really got charred."

"High amperage grabs you like a magnet. You can't let go if you try." My father made a buzzing sound. "*Bzzzzzzzt!*"

My mother snorted like she was squelching a giggle. "I never thought Tom was dumb enough to do something that stupid."

"I did. I thought he was a pinhead. But you know, it's possible he didn't cause the accident himself."

"Uh-huh. Anything's possible, I suppose. Do you think Joan might have done something? I wouldn't put it past her."

"She had plenty of reasons to. I'm sure she knew Tom kept the key to the padlock on the shed inside the junction box. Those old power tools in there were an accident waiting to happen. Maybe the accident got a little help."

"Would she know how to booby trap a power tool?"

"She could have looked it up, or asked someone. Anyway, she's all set up now."

"I hope she drops the lawsuit. I really don't want to move. This is such a good school district. It's a wonderful school system, and Andy's doing so well. He has such good friends here. It could have messed up his whole future."

"You can stop worrying. The lawsuit was all Tom's idea."

My father was right about Joan Willever dropping the lawsuit, but not about my mother being able to stop worrying. Three days into the new school year, the Oak Hills police showed up at our house in the early morning, to take my father to the station house for questioning. He told my mother to call Willard Farnsworth, the attorney they hired for the lawsuit, and have him come to the station house as quickly as possible.

At dinner, my father explained that the police investigation of Tom Willever's death had turned up a few odd coincidences that made the police suspect foul play. Tom had installed a steel flagpole on his tool shed. The base of the flagpole had come loose, and the flagpole fell against a utility pole on the rear lot line. Unfortunately for Tom, it fell on the high voltage side of the transformer box on the pole, broke a glass insulator, and made direct contact with the power line. Even more unfortunately, the loose base of the flagpole slid over, and made contact with the junction box on the shed, at the very point where some insulation was missing from the electrical cable. Tom turned on his table saw, which, as Mr. Martino had mentioned, was not grounded. Tom put his hand down on the metal table, and received over 200 milliamperes of current. The hideous burn on his arm didn't kill him. He died of cardiac arrest, probably quickly.

My father looked sweaty and twitchy. "Martino told the cops about the lawsuit. Some big mouth gossip must have told them some garbage about me and Joan. They know I work at the power company. Farnsworth told me to say nothing, and let him handle it." My father swallowed, hard. His eyes darted about. "I might be arrested. Farnsworth says they have probable cause, but not to hit the panic button yet. It's all circumstantial. No witnesses, fingerprints or other direct evidence, as far as Farnsworth can tell. There are other suspects."

He looked at me and said, "Andy, don't you worry about this." He said this to me as if not worrying about my father going to prison was something I could actually do, like he was telling me to brush my teeth.

For all the times I heard my mother casually threaten to leave my father, when the possibility that he might be taken from us reared its head, she seemed to crumble. She started talking about fleeing to Mexico, or taking other desperate measures, all of which entailed taking me out of my wonderful school system. She appeared to have serious doubts about my father's innocence, although it was possible she feigned those doubts because, logically, she could only have been certain he did not do it if she did.

At the family dinner table they joined forces, and both declared that Joan must have done it. Tom was cruel and domineering. With sixteen years of service in the Marine Corps, he had great life insurance. It was her yard, she could have been out there tinkering with the junction box in broad daylight, and no one would have thought anything of it. The Coleman Company, or the company that made the junction box, might pay off. Tom embarrassed her with his frivolous lawsuits against the neighbors. She had "motive all over the place."

I said, "What neighbors did he sue, besides us?"

My father said, "He sued the Martinos once, when their dog bit him, after he lifted the dog up by his tail. What a pinhead. To settle the lawsuit, Tom made the Martinos put the poor dog down."

"So that's why Mr. Martino called the Willevers 'suers.' Huh."

"What's that 'huh' about Andy?" said my father. "You know something?"

"The day it happened, I talked to Mr. Martino. He definitely knew the table saw wasn't grounded. He said so."

"That's good, Andy. Very good." He patted my back. "Helen, remind me to tell Farnsworth about this. The more suspects, the better."

My father's approval glowed inside me, while at the same time I felt like a tattletale. I had betrayed Mr. Martino. I didn't want to get him in trouble.

Over the next few months my parents talked several times to their attorney, the police, and the district attorney. The police and the district attorney also questioned the Martinos, Mrs. Willever, and the neighbors who lived behind the Willevers, who had the only view of the back of the tool shed. According to my dad, the cops really grilled Mr. Martino, because of the grudge about the dog, and because honest old Mr. Martino—foolishly, in my dad's opinion—admitted to knowing that Tom kept the key to the tool shed in the junction box. My parents and I spent an entire Saturday afternoon staring out the window at the police, who were poking around the tool shed. My father said the police even questioned his supervisor at work. My father said he should sue the police for harassment, but he didn't. Those months were even more stressful than July and August, when the worst things my parents had to struggle with were a private lawsuit and overlapping love triangles.

By the following summer, the investigation into Tom Willever's death seemed to lift from our lives like a morning fog. No arrests were ever made. Although the combination of flukes that came together to do in Tom seemed unlikely, there was no direct evidence against any of the suspects, and no definitive proof that it was not an accident.

I was happily back in center field for another summer vacation. Jeremy decided that he and I should be on the same team, so he let Todd Pfeiffer captain a team on the condition that he wouldn't take me if he won the bat toss. In exchange, Todd got two first picks, so he always got the only guy who could throw a fastball in the strike zone, and the only guy who could pull hit. I found I didn't mind usually being on the losing team as much as I thought I would, as long as I was teammates with my best friend.

One breezy, cool day in the summer after sixth grade Jeremy met me at the bike racks with a look of disgust on his face.

"We can't play ball today," he said. "The Oak Hills Women's Club has the whole village park reserved for a dog show. Who wants to watch a bunch of biddies with their ugly little poodles? Grown-ups are stupid."

I rode home and put my bike in the garage. My mother's station wagon was gone. I went in the house through the back screen door. As the closer eased the door shut, I heard voices coming from the basement rec room. When the latch clicked shut, the voices ceased. I went back out again, rode my bike back to the village park, and watched the dog show.

I recognized the voices. My dad and Joan Willever.

Jeremy and I drifted apart in junior high and high school. I became typically adolescent, obsessed with girls, rock music and partying. Jeremy continued being exceptionally mature for his age, drawn to politics and debating. He became a Young Republican, later a middle-aged Republican, and eventually, an old Republican.

My parents split up when I was in college. My father couldn't stay away from Joan Willever. My mother got the house, and Harry and Joan moved away from the gossiping neighbors, who never stopped speculating that one or the other of them, or both of them in concert, had murdered Tom. Joan collected Tom's life insurance. She only received nuisance value on her claim against the Coleman Tool Company, because the table saw's lack of proper grounding was not substandard at the time it was manufactured.

Jeremy taught math and computer science at a prep school in New England for thirty-five years, while I worked at 3M in St. Paul. After we retired, we occasionally talked on the phone. By then, we had very little in common. He was a conservative; I was a liberal. He was a lifetime bachelor, I had a wife, an ex-wife, and three kids. He liked classical music, I liked avant-garde jazz. But none of that mattered, because when we talked, we related exactly like we did when we were ten. We talked baseball, and told dirty jokes. *Mad* magazine didn't exist anymore, so we shared our favorite pieces from the *Onion*.

The last time we talked on the phone was a cold, rainy evening in April. Jeremy brought up, for the first time in six decades, the events of the summer of 1963.

"Whatever happened to that neighbor lady whose husband got zapped?"

"She and my dad ran off to Arizona together."

"Do tell! That must have been a surprise."

"Not really."

"You had a wicked crush on her, as I recall."

"Like father, like son."

"It probably made her even more attractive when she came into money."

"She got some life insurance. She wasn't rich."

"I would have thought she'd make a bundle on the wrongful death. You said the table saw was defective. Product liability settlements are huge windfalls. They're ruining the economy. That's the fault of the liberals."

Jeremy's political views frequently crept into his conversation.

"The table saw company wouldn't pay much," I said. "The saw was over 20 years old. In 1940 they were all made with two-prong, ungrounded plugs."

"That was stupid."

"Plus, the circumstances were so suspicious, she was lucky she wasn't prosecuted for homicide. I mean, the flagpole falls on a high voltage line and breaks the insulation. The base just happens to slide over onto the junction box right where there's bare wire on the cable? C'mon."

"Yeah, I remember you telling me about that," said Jeremy. "I guess that is pretty suspicious, especially since her husband probably wouldn't have been killed if the fuse in the table saw had blown like it's supposed to. If somebody hadn't jammed a nickel in the fuse box. Still, it's possible he was just very stupid, and very unlucky."

"Quite possible. My dad always said the guy was a pinhead."

I changed the subject to whether the Twins, who were in first place after ten games, were likely to make the playoffs. After we got off the phone, I sat up for hours, listening to the rain and sipping a snifter of brandy, while my conversation with Jeremy preyed on my mind. It has haunted me ever since.

I was absolutely certain nobody had ever said anything to me about a nickel in the fuse box, so I could not possibly have told Jeremy.

WHAT A RHUBARB!

A You-Solve-It by Laird Long

This pie-throwing wasn't done for laughs …

Maisie Cranden had only joined the St. Andrew's Church congregation four months earlier, in June, with her obedient husband Ronald. But in that short time, she'd managed to alienate the other three ladies who made up the church's Fundraising Committee, with her pompous mannerisms and highhanded criticisms and abysmal lack of fundraising skills.

At the Crafts Sale in July, she'd turned up her nose at Thelma Hemmings's beeswax candles, had commented loudly and rudely to her husband that Joyce Orlovsky's wall hangings were 'tacky,' and had dropped and broken one of Helen Kincaid's clay pots. Meanwhile, many of the woman's own dry flower arrangements had been returned by dissatisfied customers who'd complained that the flowers were so dry they turned to dust when anyone so much as walked by them.

Blithely unaware of the resentment she caused, and of her own shortcomings, Maisie had bragged to the other ladies before the September Bake Sale that, "My rhubarb pies will be snapped up before anything else—guaranteed!"

The day of the Bake Sale dawned grey and rainy. But that didn't stop the fundraising event, just moved it inside into the church basement.

"I'm here!" Maisie proclaimed, arriving barely five minutes before the sale began at 10:00 a.m. Long after she could've been, and should've been, assisting the three other committee members and the Reverend Timmins with setting up the tables and laying out the donated baked goods.

Her husband carefully set five weighty boxes down on the table closest to the door. And then Maisie scooped the pies up out of the boxes and dropped them onto the white tablecloth.

"Lumpy looking things, aren't they?" Joyce said to Thelma.

"Like their creator," Helen commented dryly. "And probably just as sour inside."

The pies were huge, with thick brown crusts that bulged ominously all over with their hidden contents. Subtly and delicacy were not Maisie Cranden's specialties.

She trotted over to the tables where Thelma, Joyce, and Helen had set out their own home-baked wares. "Hmmm," she sniffed, "brownies, fudge, and oatmeal cookies—rather bland, don't you think, ladies?"

She hustled on back to her table, as Reverend Timmins caught Helen's hand in mid-cookie toss.

Half-an-hour after the church doors had opened to the public, there was a good crowd of people in the basement sampling and buying baked goods. And then the fire alarm went off.

Reverend Timmins instantly rushed to the front of the room and expertly shepherded everyone up the stairs and out of the church. A forty-five-minute delay then ensued, while the Fire Department fruitlessly searched for smoke and flames. Finding none, they finally gave the all-clear, and Reverend Timmins ushered everybody back down into the basement.

"Aaaaah!" Maisie screamed, flinging her arms up into the air. "My pies are gone!"

The five rhubarb pies, unsold, were indeed missing from the table. The loudly distraught woman gripped Reverend Timmins's arm and pointed accusingly at her fellow Fundraising Committee members. "One of them—or all of them—stole them! Out of sheer jealousy!"

"You couldn't *give* those ugly-looking things away!" Joyce retorted.

"That's right!" Thelma chimed in. "And they probably tasted just as awful as they looked—all that green rhubarb!"

Helen added for good measure, "Those crusts were as thick as cement—they should've come with a health warning!"

Reverend Timmins managed to separate the irate women, and then he went on a search for the missing pies, accompanied by the indignant Maisie. Who screamed bloody murder a second time, when her pies were found—smashed against the stone wall in back of the church, rhubarb dripping down in long, slimy lines, heavy crusts littering the ground.

"We have to seal off the church!" Maisie shrilled. "Then interrogate everyone as to their actions and whereabouts during the time the fire alarm went off and when we were all let back into the church again! I'll telephone the police and notify the—"

"That won't be necessary, Maisie," Reverend Timmins sighed, staring at the splattered wall. "I know who threw your pies."

Solution in next month's issue …

SOLUTION TO AUGUST'S YOU-SOLVE-IT

The Corpse That Couldn't Lie by Martin Hill Ortiz

Inspector Dunsworthy summed up his evidence. "Oliver Stitz lied. Dr. Jacobs could not have said 'Paulie' or 'Polly.' Having no lips, he could not have made the 'P' sound. Dr. Jacobs did identify his killer: Oliver, or rather, Ollie. As to how he got here while avoiding the camera: that breeze from the chimney flue needs an escape to maintain such a flow. With a little inspection, we will find one of the windows ajar. Dr. Stitz, why did you cut off his lips?"

The doctor sighed. "He lied with his kisses."

9 798849 039909